DATE DUE		
AUG 1 7 2016		
AUG 1 8 2016		
JAN 2 7 2017		
MAR 2 8 2017		
MAY 0 3 2017		

Z

Also from Larissa Ione

Z

A Demonica Underworld Novella

By Larissa Ione

1001 Dark Nights

EVIL EYE
CONCEPTS

Z
A Demonica Novella
By Larissa Ione

1001 Dark Nights

Copyright 2016 Larissa Ione
ISBN: 978-1-942299-11-0

Published by Evil Eye Concepts, Incorporated

Acknowledgments

First, I want to thank my amazing readers. You are the most enthusiastic, supportive readers out there, and I love bringing this world to you.

I also want to send out huge, heartfelt thanks to Kimberly Guidroz, Pamela Jamison, and Liz Berry for all of their hard work. You ladies are absolutely incredible!

Sign up for the 1001 Dark Nights Newsletter
and be entered to win a Tiffany Key necklace.

There's a contest every month!

Go to www.1001DarkNights.com to sign up!

As a bonus, all subscribers will receive a free
1001 Dark Nights story
The First Night
by Lexi Blake & M.J. Rose

One Thousand and One Dark Nights

Once *upon a time, in the future…*

I was a student fascinated with stories and learning.
I studied philosophy, poetry, history, the occult, and
the art and science of love and magic. I had a vast
library at my father's home and collected thousands
of volumes of fantastic tales.

I learned all about ancient races and bygone
times. About myths and legends and dreams of all
people through the millennium. And the more I read
the stronger my imagination grew until I discovered
that I was able to travel into the stories… to actually
become part of them.

I wish I could say that I listened to my teacher
and respected my gift, as I ought to have. If I had, I
would not be telling you this tale now.
But I was foolhardy and confused, showing off
with bravery.

One afternoon, curious about the myth of the
Arabian Nights, I traveled back to ancient Persia to
see for myself if it was true that every day Shahryar
(Persian: شهريار, "king") married a new virgin, and then
sent yesterday's wife to be beheaded. It was written
and I had read, that by the time he met Scheherazade,
the vizier's daughter, he'd killed one thousand
women.

Something went wrong with my efforts. I arrived in the midst of the story and somehow exchanged places with Scheherazade — a phenomena that had never occurred before and that still to this day, I cannot explain.

Now I am trapped in that ancient past. I have taken on Scheherazade's life and the only way I can protect myself and stay alive is to do what she did to protect herself and stay alive.

Every night the King calls for me and listens as I spin tales. And when the evening ends and dawn breaks, I stop at a point that leaves him breathless and yearning for more. And so the King spares my life for one more day, so that he might hear the rest of my dark tale.

As soon as I finish a story... I begin a new one... like the one that you, dear reader, have before you now.

GLOSSARY

The Aegis—Society of human warriors dedicated to protecting the world from evil. Recent dissension among its ranks reduced its numbers and sent The Aegis in a new direction.

Daemani—Any being, but usually of demonic or angelic origin, who attracts the souls of the dead. Some *daemani* can block the souls from entering their bodies, while others are helpless to resist. Few *daemani* can release the souls without being in the proximity of another *daemani* or without help from a spell, a mystical item, or another being who possesses inherent or learned extraction abilities.

Emim—The wingless offspring of two fallen angels. *Emim* possess a variety of fallen angel powers, although the powers are generally weaker and more limited in scope.

Fallen Angel—Believed to be evil by most humans, fallen angels can be grouped into two categories: True Fallen and Unfallen. Unfallen angels have been cast from Heaven and are earthbound, living a life in which they are neither truly good nor truly evil. In this state, they can, rarely, earn their way back into Heaven. Or they can choose to enter Sheoul, the demon realm, in order to complete their fall and become True Fallens, taking their places as demons at Satan's side.

Harrowgate—Vertical portals, invisible to humans, which demons use to travel between locations on Earth and Sheoul. A very few beings can summon their own personal Harrowgates.

Inner Sanctum—A realm within Sheoul-gra that consists of 5 Rings, each containing the souls of demons categorized by their level of evil as defined by the Ufelskala. The Inner Sanctum is run by the fallen angel Hades and his staff of wardens, all fallen angels. Access to the Inner Sanctum is strictly limited, as the demons contained inside can take advantage of any outside object or living person in order to escape.

Memitim—Earthbound angels assigned to protect important humans called Primori. Memitim remain earthbound until they complete their duties, at which time they Ascend, earning their wings and entry into Heaven. See: Primori

Radiant—The most powerful class of Heavenly angel in existence, save Metatron. Unlike other angels, Radiants can wield unlimited power in all realms and can travel freely through Sheoul, with very few exceptions. The designation is awarded to only one angel at a time. Two can never exist simultaneously, and they cannot be destroyed except by God or Satan. The fallen angel equivalent is called a Shadow Angel. See: Shadow Angel

Shadow Angel—The most powerful class of fallen angel in existence, save Satan and Lucifer. Unlike other fallen angels, Shadow Angels can wield unlimited power in all realms, and they possess the ability to gain entrance into Heaven. The designation is awarded to only one angel at a time, and they can never exist without their equivalent, a Radiant. Shadow Angels cannot be destroyed except by God or Satan. The Heavenly angel equivalent is called a Radiant. See: Radiant.

Sheoul—Demon realm. Located on its own plane deep in the bowels of the Earth, accessible to most only by Harrowgates and hellmouths.

Sheoul-gra—A holding tank for demon souls. A realm that exists independently of Sheoul, it is overseen by Azagoth, also known as the Grim Reaper. Within Sheoul-gra is the Inner Sanctum, where demon souls go to be kept in torturous limbo until they can be reborn.

Sheoulic—Universal demon language spoken by all, although many species also speak their own language.

Ufelskala—A scoring system for demons, based on their degree of evil. All supernatural creatures and evil humans can be categorized into the five Tiers, with the Fifth Tier comprising of the worst of the wicked.

Chapter One

Inside Sheoul, the demon realm sometimes called Hell, evil was everywhere.

It dripped off the sides of the sheer rock walls in streaks of black acid that ate into the stone with a hiss. It wafted through the humid air on tendrils of mist that reeked of sulfur and decaying flesh. And, as Vex watched, it oozed like toothpaste from out of a fissure in midair that only people like her could see.

Her purple-tipped black hair, already short and spiky, stood even more on end as the thing squeezing out of the fissure, a dead demon's soul, popped free of whatever realm and mystical enclosure it had been inside. The toothpastey glob took a transparent, vaguely humanoid shape, but its glowing crimson eyes were sharp and clear. A malevolent wave of rage and hate rolled off the soul, and Vex backed away, even though escape was impossible for her.

She was what her parents had called a *daemani*, a demon soul magnet, a person to whom souls stuck like glue. According to them, most *daemanis* couldn't prevent it from happening, and that was a serious pain in the ass. If a demon died near Vex, not even the Grim Reaper's personal *daemanis*, creatures called *griminions*, had a chance to collect the soul before it got sucked into her and stored as a glyph on her skin.

The demon shrieked, a sound only she or another soul-sensitive person could hear, as it struggled to keep from being sucked into the prison of her body. In a futile attempt to avoid the inevitable, she fled, her booted feet nimbly negotiating the rock shard-strewn ground that was all too common in this part of Sheoul.

But no matter how fast she ran, every time she looked over her shoulder, the distance between her and the soul had decreased. Closer. Closer. Oh, shit—

A fireball of pain exploded against her lower spine, knocking her off her feet and sending her tumbling down a ravine infested with thick, thorny vines that tore at her exposed flesh and nearly ripped her knapsack off her back. But it was the misery of the soul settling in that left tears streaming down her face.

Agony, like a million hellfire ants crawling beneath her skin, wracked her as she scrambled to her feet and clawed her way back to the trail. The demon inside her tore at her mind, shrieking at a maddeningly high pitch that made her gut twist.

"Female." The deep, serrated voice startled her, and it must have startled her newest hitchhiking soul too, because the demon spirit stopped freaking out, giving her a chance to catch her breath.

Palming one of the blades hidden in her boot, she shoved to her feet and stared up at the massive armored demon. He had to be at least eight feet tall, with horns poking up through the matte black helmet. Mahogany skin stretched tight on the only exposed parts of his body, his long, clawed hands and his craggy face. She grimaced in oral hygiene horror as his cracked lips peeled back from crooked and rotten—but sharp—teeth and five-inch tusks.

"Who are you?" The symbol etched into the shoulder piece of his armor marked him as a servant of the necromancer she'd come to see, but someone had been trying to kill her for months, and until she knew who they were and why they wanted her dead, she had to be extra careful.

"I am Othog," he growled. "You are here to see the great and horrible Frank?"

The word Frank supposedly meant something really scary in some obscure demon language, but Vex had to struggle to keep a straight face.

"Yes," she said, concealing the blade in her palm. She'd already picked a vulnerable chink in his armor to slide the blade through if the guy pulled any shit. "I'm here to see the...Frank."

He made a sweeping gesture with his arm, and his armor creaked like nails on a chalkboard. "This way."

Demons weren't the most trustworthy folk, so she kept her weapon ready as she followed him down a well-worn path she swore hadn't been there before. Bony hands punched through the vegetation, grabbing at them, and random puddles of what she could only assume was steaming blood formed and dissipated as they trudged along the trail. After what seemed like hours but was probably only a few minutes, they reached a passageway that led deep into the side of a mountain. Pulsing veins ran along the dark walls, as if the mountain itself was alive. Maybe it was. Sheoul was weird and dangerous, which was why she'd chosen to live in the human world.

Not that humans weren't also weird and dangerous, but as a supernatural being she had little to worry about from weakling mortals.

A few dozen yards ahead, an orange glow emanated from an opening in the mountain, and as they got closer, the air went from humid and hot to humid and searing. At the end of the passage, around a corner framed by fang-shaped pillars as tall as a skyscraper, she stopped dead, her jaw falling open.

A massive chamber had been built as a hive-like structure, with holes carved into the sheer walls where bizarre, insect-like demons skittered between them. What she assumed were hollowed-out tunnels crisscrossed the space overhead, running like connective tissue from wall to wall.

"The great and horrible Frank is there." Othog gestured to a dude who could have been her escort's twin, except that Frank was taller. And bigger. And his horns were caked with blood and bits of dried flesh.

Charming. She *really* did not like demons.

Squaring her shoulders, she strode across the hard-packed floor, kicking aside old bones and skulls that littered the area. Frank stood near a bubbling vat the size of a wine barrel, his hands moving through the sickly greenish-brown vapor that rose from the boiling liquid.

"Excuse me, sir," she said politely. Demons like him expected arrogant displays of alpha bullshit, so she always looked for ways to throw them off or make them underestimate her. "I'm here to see you."

He turned to her, his lips stretching into a grotesque grin. "An *emim*," he said, his enormous tusks making his words sound like drunken slurs. "I haven't seen one of your kind in centuries."

How he knew she was an *emim*, the offspring of two fallen angels, she had no idea. Didn't really matter, she supposed. "Yes, I'm quite special," she said dryly. "Now, if we could just get down to business."

"You have something to offer me."

"Souls," she said. "I have four...no, five...souls to sell. One is at least a Tier Four on the Ufelskala and worth more than the other four combined—"

He hissed. "Shut up, *soul scavenger*." His beady eyes shifted to the nearest demon besides Othog, a wrinkly, fat creature with what looked like metal spikes sticking out of its leathery face. Frank lowered his voice. "Do not speak of such things."

"First of all," she said, keeping her voice low, but she couldn't hide her irritation at having been called a soul scavenger. "The politically correct term for what I am is *daemani*. Second, I have souls to unload, and no one is buying anymore. I'm willing to give them to you at a fifty percent discount. Half a million each for the four weakest. Three million for all of them. That's a hell of a deal, if you'll excuse the pun." The dude didn't crack a smile at all. Tough crowd. "I was told you might need them."

"Oh, I need them." His snout-like nose wrinkled. "But not enough to risk my own soul."

Argh! This was so frustrating. Not just frustrating, but terrifying. The demons inside her fought constantly, were in a never-ending battle to see who could try to possess her. Fortunately, none of the souls were very strong or evil...except the one that had attacked her a few minutes ago.

That one needed to go, and fast. "What is going on? Why is everyone suddenly so afraid to deal in souls?"

The demon reached into the bubbling brew and plucked out what looked like a finger. Demons were so disgusting. And he'd had the nerve to insult *her*. For the millionth time, she thanked her parents for raising her in the human realm.

"Because those who buy and sell souls are being slaughtered," he said as he popped the finger into his mouth.

Well, that explained why half of the people who usually bought from her were missing and the other half refused to see her. "By who?"

"Unclear." A piece of...gah...a fingernail...hung out of the corner of his mouth. "There are rumors that Satan wants all souls for himself, but that doesn't make sense, not when he's never taken issue with the soul market before."

Othog, cleared his throat. "Some say Satan was destroyed by Archangels who are now ruling Sheoul."

"Bullshit," Frank said. The piece of finger was still there, jiggling as his scaly lips moved. "Angels couldn't mount that kind of attack on Satan. Not inside Sheoul, and not without us hearing about it."

"Then what's your theory?" she asked. There had been rumors floating around for months about a possible new ruler in Sheoul, but she hadn't believed any of them. After all, who could overthrow Satan?

Frank's forked tongue snaked out to catch the little bit of fingernail, and she swallowed bile, trying desperately not to gag. "I've heard whispers that someone named Revenant is sitting on the throne. I know nothing about him, but if my sources are correct, he's a traitor who betrayed Satan."

No demon was powerful enough to wrest control from Satan. Which meant this Revenant person could only be one thing. "Is he a fallen angel?"

Frank picked his teeth with one long claw. "Some say he's a Shadow Angel."

She whistled under her breath. A Shadow Angel, according to legend, was the most powerful class of fallen angel in existence. Only Satan, and maybe Lucifer, were more powerful. Although she'd heard that Lucifer had been destroyed by one of the Four Horsemen of the Apocalypse.

Which was ludicrous. The Four Horsemen were myths, and Lucifer probably was as well. Heck, the only reason she believed in Satan was that her parents were once angels, and if they said he existed, then he probably did.

"Look, I guess it really doesn't matter what he is or if he even exists. I need to sell these souls." Actually, she just needed to release them. The problem was that they couldn't be released without another, equally powerful soul magnet around, otherwise they just got sucked back into her. "Give me a name. Any name."

"There is only one." Frank bared his never-seen-a-toothbrush teeth, and his voice went low and ominous. "And his name...is Azagoth."

She had a feeling she was supposed to be surprised or in awe or something. "Who the hell is Azagoth?"

Frank gestured to his crony without answering her question. "He will take you to the entrance to Azagoth's realm."

Realm? The guy had his own *realm*? "Wait." She shrugged away from Othog. "I want to know who this guy is."

"He is someone I would not want to face."

Great. If the most powerful necromancer in the Ghul region of Sheoul didn't want to face this Azagoth person, she didn't want to, either. But she was desperate, both for money and to rid herself of her newest passenger on the soul train, so she allowed Othog to escort her to a Harrowgate that took them to a circle of stones deep in the Russian wilderness.

"A drop of blood in the center should grant you access." Othog disappeared into the forest, practically melting into the foliage, before she could ask any questions.

Okay, well, she had to get this done. She jabbed the tip of her finger with one of her blades and stepped close to the circle. But just as she was about to cross the stone line, the hair on the back of her neck stood up, and even before she heard a voice, she knew she wasn't alone.

"*Emim*. Let me kill her."

In a single, smooth motion, she drew twin blades from the sheathes at her hip and spun around to face the newcomers. Two big dudes in black hooded robes stood there, their ageless, remarkably handsome faces telling her little except that they probably got a lot of ass.

They had swords at their backs, but something told her these two were more than lethal without the blades. She was an expert fighter, but the power she sensed coming from the hooded dudes left her in the dust.

Under her skin, the demon souls writhed, agitated by the presence of the newcomers.

"Who are you?"

The rude assholes didn't answer, but when their magnificent feathered wings flared, she knew. Angels. So. Much. Shit.

The angel on the left, the one who had spoken, lunged at her, but she was ready. She dropped and rolled, kicking out her foot to catch him in the knee.

"Leave her!" Right Angel's voice rang out, and a split second later, heat exploded near her head and she was thrown to the dirt. For a moment, she thought she was dead. But then she was yanked to her feet by a vicious hand around the back of her neck.

"What the hell?" Left Angel peeled himself off the ground, his robes smoking, his eyes burning with anger as he glared at Right Angel from under the hood. "Why did you protect her?"

"Because she's carrying souls." Right Angel squeezed her neck, stopping her from stomping on his foot. "If you kill her, they escape. We need to take her to Azagoth."

"Oh, bloody hell," she snapped. "That's what I was trying to do when you bastards attacked me for no fucking reason."

"Why are you going to see him?" Right Angel shoved her into the center of the stone circle, his hand still clamped around her neck. "Did he summon you?"

"Did he *summon* me? Why would he summon me? I don't even know who this Azagoth idiot is."

Left Angel gaped at her like she was a complete moron. "He's the Keeper of Souls, you vile demon dimwit. You're going to see the Grim Reaper."

Chapter Two

Being the Grim Reaper's second-in-command wasn't the worst job in the world, but as Zhubaal listened to the bloodcurdling screams coming from the room at the end of the shadowy hallway, he was reminded that it wasn't the best job in the world, either.

However, it *was* a necessary one if he ever hoped to find his beloved Laura, whose soul had once been trapped here in Sheoul-gra, the Alcatraz of demon, fallen angel, and evil human souls. She'd been here for decades until, thirty years ago, she was paroled—reborn—her soul ensconced in a new body. Zhubaal had been searching for her new identity ever since, but so far he hadn't had any luck tracking her down.

He would, though. The oaths that bound them to each other were unbreakable. Pure. And he was tenacious as shit.

He *would* find her.

"Damn." Razr, a fallen angel who Azagoth had recently appointed to act as Zhubaal's own second-in-command, came up next to Z and stared at their boss's office door. "Who's in there with him?"

Z cast a sideways glance at the guy who, as usual, wore plain brown monk-like robes and flip-flops. Why he dressed like that, Zhubaal had no idea. Razr refused to talk about it no matter how drunk Z got him. "Some Orphmage who has incredibly bad judgment and thought he could blackmail the Grim Reaper."

"Shit." Razr rubbed his tattooed, bald head. "You're gonna make me clean up the mess, aren't you?"

Grinning, Zhubaal clapped him on the back. "Quit whining. This should be the last one today—" He broke off as a sharp, tingly sensation washed over him in a wave that was almost...sexual.

Not that he knew what a sexual wave felt like. Not really.

Sure, he experienced desire like every normal fallen angel, but lonely orgasms weren't exactly anything to get excited about.

And this particular wave definitely didn't mean an orgasm was impending. It meant that someone had activated the portal connecting Sheoul-gra to one of several portals in the earthly realm.

A visitor was inbound, and the intense residual electric current pulsing through his veins meant the newcomer wasn't your average lowlife demon begging for an audience with the person in charge of reincarnating souls. Which also meant whoever was about to show up was probably an egomaniacal douchebag.

Razr felt it too, and he barked out a laugh. "Bet you wish you were the one getting to clean Orphmage bits off Azagoth's walls now, huh?"

No, but only barely. He wasn't in the mood to deal with some arrogant demon or holy-rolling angel who reminded him of who he used to be. Not when he'd just learned his latest lead on Laura's reincarnated identity had fallen through.

Shooting Razr the finger, Zhubaal exited the building and took the stone steps down to the courtyard two at a time. The fountain in the center sprayed a fine mist over his bare arms as he hurried past it to the portal platform that sat like a miniature helicopter landing pad twenty yards away.

A column of white light struck from out of the featureless gray sky above, and when it cleared, two angels he recognized stood inside the stone circle on the portal pad. He had no idea who the weapons-heavy female with the short black hair with them was, but she was as pissed as a wet cat being held by its scruff.

The angel, who Z knew only by the code name Jim Bob, had his hand wrapped around the back of her neck, forcing her to walk on the tiptoes of her thigh-high boots as they stepped off the platform. Every time she reached for one of the weapons stashed around her body in various holsters, he swatted her hand away as if she were no more bothersome than a gnat.

Jim Bob shoved her forward. "We found this... creature... attempting to break through the portal."

The female's violet eyes burned with fury. She was pretty, in a dangerous sort of way, which only made her prettier. Oh, she wasn't Zhubaal's type; he'd always gone for females with less makeup, fewer weapons, and more clothes. But that didn't mean he couldn't appreciate a smoking hot female who looked like she could chew him up and swallow too.

As if you know what that would be like.

"I wasn't trying to break through." She lashed out with her foot and kicked Jim Bob in the shin, but he didn't even flinch. Then again, he was twice her size and built like a tank. "I was trying to activate the portal. You know, like a normal person. You feathered morons interrupted."

Jim Bob yanked her off her feet and held her at arm's length, like one might do with a sewer rat. "She's *emim*." He sneered, baring his teeth. "I can practically smell the wrongness of her."

"Gee, asshole," she growled, still doing her best to kick him, "why don't you tell us how you really feel about my kind."

The other angel, a raven-haired pretty-boy code named Ricky Bobby, snorted. "Your kind should be destroyed. Fallen angels are traitorous scum who weren't meant to breed. They and their *emim* offspring deserve to be slaughtered."

What a tool. If Zhubaal were anywhere but here, he'd lob a ball of acid fire at Ricky Bobby's haloed head. "You know I'm a fallen angel, right?" He gestured to himself. "I mean, I'm standing right here."

Jim Bob and Ricky Bobby stared, completely unmoved. Holier-than-thou pricks. Literally holier, since they were actual Heavenly angels and Z was one of those traitorous scum who wasn't meant to breed.

He sighed, tired of dealing with two angels who couldn't be *too* angelic if they were associating with the Grim Reaper. "Release the female. I'll take it from here. Razr is inside. He'll show you to Azagoth's office." He reconsidered that, thinking that Azagoth's office wouldn't be presentable for a while. "Or the library."

Jim Bob opened his fist and dropped the female to the ground. "I can find Azagoth on my own."

"You know the rules, Jim Bob," Z said as the female leaped to her feet and glared at the two angels. "Outsider dickbags can't roam around without an escort."

Jim Bob's eyes flashed pure white, twin bolts of divine lightning, and Zhubaal wondered if the guy was actually capable of bypassing Azagoth's power-dampening spell and delivering a damaging strike. He didn't know Jim Bob's true identity or what kind of angel he was, but one thing was certain; the angel was powerful. Even here in Sheoulgra, where everyone but Azagoth was limited in the use of their inherent supernatural abilities, Jim Bob exuded danger. And arrogance.

He was definitely high up on the angelic food chain.

The asshole.

"Don't even think about it, angel." Zhubaal's fallen angel wings erupted from his back as he summoned one of the few powers Azagoth allowed, a dark shield of evil energy capable of temporarily disrupting any Heavenly energy that struck it. "I have more power here than you do."

A slow smile spread across Jim Bob's face. "Do you really think so?"

"Want to test me?"

For a long moment, Z was sure the guy was going to attack. But even as the air between them crackled, Jim Bob's eyes went back to normal. "One day. But today I don't have time to kick your ass. I will see Azagoth *now*."

With that, he strode toward the building, extending his massive white wings in a dismissive fuck-you gesture. The chickenshit. Ricky Bobby went with him, giving off his own powerful vibe and a rude flap of dove gray wings. He'd only been here with Jim Bob twice, and he hadn't spoken a word until today. Zhubaal hoped he'd go back to dickish silence for future visits.

"Those guys are major assholes," the female muttered.

Zhubaal tucked away his leathery wings, still hating how naked they felt without Heavenly feathers even after all these years. He'd eventually sprout feathers, assuming he survived a few centuries, but they'd likely be ugly, malformed, twisted by evil.

"Angels generally are." Zhubaal turned to her, amused to find her glaring at the angels' backs while fingering the hilt of a blade at her leather-clad hip as if fantasizing about plunging it into their skulls. He'd like to see that. She'd die, of course, but hey, at least Z had Razr around to clean up the mess.

Still, it would be a shame to see her slaughtered. Not many *emim* made their way down here to seek an audience with Azagoth, especially not ones who looked like she did.

He let his gaze drop from her rounded hips to her slender thighs, where her ripped black leggings disappeared into purple-laced midnight boots with stiletto heels. How the hell did she fight in those things?

He dragged his gaze back up, admiring her flat, bare midriff and the leather top that was little more than a bra covering ample breasts. *Barely* covering ample breasts. Her short black hair, dyed purple at the spiky tips, teased the shell of her ears, and damn it all, his mouth watered with the desire to take the lobes between his teeth and make her purr.

And what the hell? He never fantasized about females like this. His focus had been on no one but Laura since before he fell, and even the one foray into experimentation he'd taken with Cat last year had been more about seeing if he was still functional than anything.

Or maybe he'd just been lonely. A hundred years without so much as a kiss was a long freaking time.

"You like what you see?" She sauntered toward him with slow, deliberate steps. Somehow, her spiked heels didn't wobble on the uneven ground no matter how hard her hips popped with each step. "Do you?"

Why, yes. Yes, he did like what he saw. But she hadn't chosen such a sexy outfit for Z's benefit and he knew it. "You're wasting your time with me, and if you're planning to seduce Azagoth, you should know he has a mate. And Lilliana does *not* share."

She stopped a couple of feet away, her fingers still fondling the blade. Which shouldn't be erotic but somehow was. "I'm not here for that."

No doubt seducing Azagoth wasn't her primary goal, but he knew her kind, knew her racy clothes were tools she'd use if she needed to. And something about Azagoth got all the females—and males, for that matter—worked up. Once she laid eyes on him, she'd try to seduce him. They all did.

"What's your name? And what is your business with Azagoth?" Stepping closer, he lowered his voice and looked down at her from his extra foot of height. "And keep in mind that I'm his gatekeeper. You *will* tell me or you won't get off this platform."

She coyly fingered the plunging neckline of her top and batted her jewel-toned eyes. "I'm Vex, and I have a proposition for your boss."

"I'm Zhubaal, and I need a little more than that." He narrowed his eyes, refusing to be charmed or seduced. But damn, she really did have nice breasts. "What kind of proposition?"

For a long moment she stared up at him, her ruby lips pressed together in a stubborn line of silence. Just as he was about to send her back to whatever realm she'd come from, she gave up the seductress BS and held out her right arm.

"See these glyphs?" She traced the outline of one of five squiggly black circles with the tip of one amethyst-painted fingernail. "Touch one."

"If this is a trick—"

"How stupid do you think I am?" she snapped. "If Azagoth is really the Grim Reaper, he's one of the most powerful beings in the universe. Do you honestly think I'm here to piss him off by screwing with one of his *griminions*?"

Well, that was insulting. "I'm not a *griminion*," he ground out. "*Griminions* are ugly little freaks who collect souls when a demon or evil human dies. I'm just your standard everyday *minion*."

She rolled her eyes. "I know. I was being funny. You're the *Grim* Reaper's minion. *Griminion*." She nudged him with her arm. "Come on. Touch me."

Anxious to be rid of this obnoxious female, he gripped her wrist and pressed his fingers against two—or maybe three—of the circles.

He had no idea how many of the things he touched because the moment his skin came into contact with them, the powerful burn of sheer evil shot through him and knocked the breath from his lungs. Holy hell, what were those glyphs? Malevolence seared his skin and forced superheated blood to flow like lava through his veins as he released her and stumbled backward, his head spinning.

"They're souls," Vex said, her voice cutting through his agony.

"That's what you're feeling. They attached themselves to me, and I think Azagoth might want to take them off my hands."

The overwhelming evil drained rapidly away now that he was no longer touching the glyphs, but another sensation remained, one that once again took away his breath and left him shaken.

Familiarity. Comfort. Love.

Was it...possible? He knew the warmth of this, the desperate need to hold onto it, but the sensation was fading with every spastic beat of his heart.

Laura.

His fingers cramped, and he looked down to see that he was clutching his chest as if he could dig through his ribs to his racing heart.

He licked his dry lips and tried to summon enough moisture in his mouth to speak. He was afraid to hope, afraid to ask the question that sat on the tip of his parched tongue. But he had to. This was why he'd willingly fallen from grace all those decades ago. The reason he'd begged the Archangel Uriel to slice off his coveted maroon wings, coveted not so much for the color as for what they represented.

The best of the best.

Now he lived among the worst of the worst.

"Do you know who the souls belonged to?" he asked, deliberately spacing out his words so he didn't run his tongue like a kid hopped up on Halloween candy. "When they were in physical form, I mean."

She shook her head. "They don't speak to me." Pained shadows flickered in Vex's eyes, and he wondered what the souls were doing to her. He'd barely touched them and they'd given him a body migraine, but they were melded into her flesh. "Not with words."

He didn't need words. He stared at Vex's arm, at the thin, swirly lines that marked her skin, and he knew.

One of the souls in Vex's body belonged to his beloved. One of the souls was Laura.

Chapter Three

Vex stared at Zhubaal, but only because *he* was staring at *her*. Staring like she'd suddenly sprouted a halo.

But during the stare-off, she discovered that the blond, dark-eyed fallen angel was outrageously hot. Absolutely delicious in black jeans, combat boots, and a navy T-shirt that clung to a hard, muscular body. If she'd met him anyplace other than the Grim Reaper's freaking realm, she'd be testing the sexual promise that wrapped around him like a second skin.

But as it was, he not only seemed uninterested, he seemed shocked, or maybe horrified, by her.

"What's your deal?" she finally snapped. "What is it humans say? Take a picture, it'll last longer?"

"The souls," he said roughly. "You claim they speak to you, but not with words."

"That's not exactly what I said, but that's the gist." The souls vibrated, as if reminding her why she was here. They were probably as anxious to be free of her as she was of them. "Now, do I get to see the Grim Reaper or not?"

And if so, how could she work this to her advantage? She needed to sell these souls, but meeting the Grim Reaper was also a once-in-a-lifetime chance she couldn't let slip by. She was tired of being treated like a scavenger. Collecting souls paid well, but in the demon world, she was considered as loathsome as humans considered drug dealers.

Working with the Grim Reaper would give her legitimacy as well as protection from the people who were destroying the underworld soul trade.

Zhubaal hesitated, but after a moment he jerked his head in a "follow me" motion and started toward one of the big buildings at the edge of what appeared to an ancient Greek city. She held back for a few heartbeats to get a good look at how well those jeans fit. *Niiice.*

"How do they communicate with you?" he called back to her. "The souls, I mean."

She caught up to him, her heels clacking on the cobblestones. "Um, they don't. I sense them. Like, I can feel how evil they are." She held up her arm. "Four of these feel like Tier Ones and Twos on the Ufelskala. But the other one...the newest one..." She shuddered. "The evil is as strong as anything I've ever felt."

It was stronger even than the soul that had possessed her years ago, that had sent her on a rampage through regions of Sheoul where she was no longer welcome. The nightmares from those two weeks of hell left her exhausted and emotionally drained far too often, but it was nothing compared to the guilt that ate at her every day.

She had to get rid of this soul and fast. She couldn't go through that again. She wouldn't. She'd kill herself before she allowed another evil being to use her body for slaughter and mayhem.

Zhubaal stopped so suddenly she whacked her shoulder against his arm. It was like running into a wall. A hard, tall, do-me-against-it wall.

"Do the souls interact?" he asked. "Can the strong ones torment the weaker ones?"

What an odd question. "Yes. Why? How is this relevant to my meeting with Azagoth?"

"Everything is relevant when it comes to Azagoth." He started walking again, taking her past a perfectly trimmed hedgerow separating the mansion's grounds from the other buildings, a sparkling fountain, and several Greek statues and seemingly random pillars that didn't support anything.

This was *not* what she'd expected to see in a realm run by the Grim Reaper.

Zhubaal led her up a stone staircase that ran the entire width of the building. "How is it that you collect the souls?"

"It's hard to explain." As they approached the giant doors, they swung open. "I'm a sort of magnet. They call people like me *daemani*, but if your boss deals in souls, he'll probably know that. If there's a nonhuman, supernatural soul in the area, it will find me."

"How? *Griminions* appear within seconds of a demon's death."

"They're too late if I'm the one who killed the demon or a demon dies near me." She made a habit out of not killing demons if she didn't have to, but shit happened because demons were assholes, and a lot of them deserved to die. "Once I visited a friend at Underworld General, and in the hour I was there, two demon souls got sucked inside me. Two! Those doctors must be terrible if they can't keep anyone alive. But now, if I need some fast cash, I take a stroll through the hospital." Well, not anymore. Not since the soul market crashed.

He gave her a judgey sideways glance. "I would keep that to yourself. Azagoth considers all souls to be his. If he knows you intentionally stole them out from under him, you'll pay with your own soul."

Azagoth was a greedy bastard, wasn't he? She'd keep that opinion to herself, too.

Zhubaal led her inside the building. She squinted in the torch-lit darkness, and holy freak show, they'd walked into a nightmare museum of statues. *This* was what she'd expected to see in a realm run by the Grim Reaper.

In a room that was seemingly endless, rows of life-sized stone figures of demons of all species were on display, all in various states of agony. Skulls and weapons lined the walls, some of the weapons buried *in* the skulls. Vex had been inside some seriously creepy and haunting places, many filled with bloody horrors she couldn't even describe. But something about this room was more disturbing than a room full of blatant gore.

Maybe the creep-factor came from the feeling that she was being watched.

"These are living statues." Zhubaal's boots thundered as he strode through the cavernous room. "Sometimes Azagoth doesn't kill his enemies."

Horror slithered down her spine as what Zhubaal said sank in. She gave a wide berth to an eyeless Silas demon that seemed to be reaching for her, its face twisted in misery.

"How long have they been like this?" Her voice sounded small in this place, and she didn't know if it was a trick of the space or if she really sounded like she wanted to be anywhere but here.

Zhubaal high-fived an elf-like Neethul statue as they walked past, and she wondered how aware the demons were of the world around them. "Some are new, within the last few decades, but most are hundreds, if not thousands of years old."

They'd been trapped for *thousands of years?*

The souls on her arm began to tingle as if frightened, growing into a violent vibration that became more intense the farther inside they went. The super evil soul, which she would now dub SuperEvil, began to claw at her. The souls always got antsy when she was near another soul magnet, but this seemed more like fear than the usual eagerness to get out of her body, even though the next host could enslave it, eat it, use it for spells...souls were all-purpose items that used to net a fortune.

She did the whole Lamaze thing through the psychic assault, but when Zhubaal narrowed his eyes, she stopped breathing like she was giving birth and smiled as if nothing was wrong. Once he turned away, she went back to Lamaze...just more quietly.

They finally exited the statue room, and just as they turned down a long, dimly lit hallway, the douche-bro angels brushed past them on their way out, barely sparing a scornful glance at them. Steps behind, a bald guy in a shapeless brown monk robe followed, presumably the angels' escort.

A dark-haired male in black slacks and a button-down shirt the color of dried blood emerged from a doorway at the end of the hall. The souls inside her freaked the hell out, vibrating so hard she thought her skin might come right off her body. They wanted her to run, to get away from here, and frankly, it was tempting.

Breathe. Don't let them see you as anything less than someone in perfect control.

"Z," the guy said, his deep voice as intensely captivating as his emerald eyes. This was Azagoth. No doubt about it. "I'm heading to the Inner Sanctum. You're in charge until I get back." He scowled, and his head whipped around to her so fast it was a blur. "Who are you?"

The souls screamed. They screamed so loud that for the first time, she heard them. Actually heard them and felt their fear. Not that she could blame them. Azagoth was terrifying, made all the more worse by his beauty. He was tall, dark, handsome, and he exuded danger that left her cold inside. Not even Tier Five demons could match this kind of soul-sucking cold.

"I'm Vex." Somehow she managed to not sound like a cornered mouse.

He turned back to Zhubaal as if he hadn't spoken to her at all. "I'll see her when I return."

Zhubaal's hand snapped out to catch Azagoth's arm as he started past him. "But my Lord—"

Azagoth turned his gaze on her once again, and her blood froze. "When. I. Return."

No! Run away! Escape! The souls shrieked, clawed, tore at her mind, even as Azagoth strode away. And it was then that she realized that this was the first time it had ever happened.

The souls didn't want out. They wanted to stay in.

* * * *

Dammit. Z hadn't been able to talk to Azagoth about his suspicion regarding Vex and the souls she carried. One soul in particular.

Oh, he could have tried, but he knew Azagoth, and the guy had been on the edge of an explosion. About what, Z had no idea. All he knew was that you didn't want to get caught in one of the Grim Reaper's concussive blasts. When that guy detonated, he went nuclear.

"What now?" Vex asked, and he wasn't surprised to hear the slightest tremor in her voice. But her violet eyes were hard, the eyes of a warrior, and if Azagoth frightened her, it didn't show. Impressive, especially for an *emim*, most of whom wielded very few of the abilities their more powerful fallen angel parents possessed. "I can't leave. One of the souls inside me is dangerous."

He lowered his voice as a resident Unfallen walked past on his way to the kitchens. "Dangerous how?"

"If a soul is powerful enough, *and* evil enough, it can possess me."

Vex spoke with a flippant wave of her hand that didn't match up with the way her fingers trembled. "It's not a pleasant experience. Weaker souls generally team up to keep more sinister ones at bay, but this one is crazy strong. Its malevolence is…I dunno, pure, I guess. I don't know how long I can last against it."

A chill crawled up Z's spine at the thought that Laura was trapped inside Vex with a malevolent demon. He'd met a handful of *daemani* in his life, but he'd never asked them questions about their abilities, let alone if the souls they packed around hung out together.

"What do you mean, pure?" He started back through the statue room to leave the building, and he got a kick at how she walked so fast he had to pick up his pace to keep up.

"The souls all have different…vibes. I can get a general sense of how old they are and how many lives they've lived." She grimaced at the statue of a genocidal Darquethoth scumbag Azagoth had impaled before encasing him in stone to suffer death pangs for all eternity. "Each life seems to mellow them out, for lack of a better word. But those who spend a long time living a single life…they tend to be really fucking strong. I'd bet that whoever I picked up today is either ancient or infected with great evil, and they definitely have a thirst for pain and death." She cast him a brief, impish smile. "And sex. So it's not all bad. But this soul is very, very angry."

He wondered if Laura's second life had "mellowed" her, although he couldn't see how. As an angel, she'd been the epitome of serenity, preferring to listen rather than talk, to negotiate for peace rather than fight. Those were the very qualities that had gotten her banished from their angelic warrior Order and led to her fall from Heaven.

Holy shit, after all these years of looking, was it really possible that he was this close to finally seeing his betrothed again? Did she know he was close? Or was she too busy trying to escape the evil soul inside Vex?

He slowed while the doors swung open. "Can the angry soul harm the others?"

Please say no.

"Yes." She practically ran outside, and he swore she breathed a sigh of relief when the doors closed behind them. "I can feel their pain even now."

The Ipsylum warrior in him rose up in eagerness to destroy whoever was hurting Laura, followed by frustration that there was no enemy to fight. "Can you stop it from happening?"

She paused on a step to look at him like he was crazy. "Um, no. Why? Don't tell me a big, bad fallen angel is worried about some poor little demon souls being bullied."

He couldn't care less about any souls but one. Laura had been so kind and gentle before her fall from grace, and even after, as a fallen angel, she hadn't changed much. But, as Azagoth had pointed out, she'd been killed before her soul could become too corrupted by evil. She'd also been Unfallen, an angel who had lost her wings but hadn't entered Hell in order to complete her fall and allow darkness to flood her soul. She'd been decent, even until the end, and it made him sick to think that she could, right now, be suffering in ways he couldn't even comprehend.

He ignored Vex's ridiculous question and walked her around the hedgerow. "This way."

"Where are we going? You didn't answer me about what we're doing now."

They turned down a cobblestone path that bisected a vast, grassy lawn that used to be nothing but scorched wasteland before Azagoth's mate, Lilliana, worked some kind of voodoo on his shriveled, blackened, Grinchy heart.

"Now," he said, "you get to check in to Sheoul-gra's finest luxury hotel."

One black brow arched. "Sheoul-gra's finest what?"

He gestured ahead, toward the buildings that spread out like wings behind Azagoth's great mansion, all laid out in replica of ancient Athens. "The one with the gargoyle pillars and the skull carved above the entry. I call it Motel 666."

"Clever. And just begging to be the site of a massacre." She rubbed her arm absently, and he wondered which of the glyphs belonged to Laura. She was *so* close, and it killed him to not be able to touch her. "So you're serious? You have a hotel?"

"They're more like what humans call dormitories."

"Dormitories?" A breeze ruffled her spiky locks as she glanced around. "For who?"

"I'll show you." He led her to the back of the building, which opened up into a courtyard where several dozen people sparred with various weapons under the barked instruction of fallen angels. "Unfallen and Memitim."

She frowned. "Unfallen are fallen angels who haven't entered Sheoul, right? They can still be redeemed. But what's a Memitim?"

Lilliana waved from across the courtyard where she was talking to three of their newest Unfallen arrivals. Ever since Azagoth turned Sheoul-gra into a sanctuary for Unfallen looking for a chance to redeem themselves and earn their way back into Heaven, they'd seen a steady stream of new faces.

"They're all Azagoth's children," he said. "They're a special class of earthbound angel born to protect certain humans and earn their wings."

"Unfallen and Memitim," she mused. "Two sides of the same coin. One group was born with everything to gain, and the other was born with everything to lose."

His head whipped around to her. That was something Laura would have said. She always looked for the commonalities in people rather than the differences. It was another of the traits that had led to her being shunned by their Ipsylum Order. The thought irritated the twin scars where his luxurious wings that marked him as an elite warrior class had been sliced off. It had taken two years after his fall to grow his fallen angel wings which, while studier and more resistant to fire than his old wings, were inferior and uglier in every other way.

"What *is* your deal?" Vex rounded on him, one of those lethal heels grinding on the stone path. "Why do you keep staring at me?" She batted her eyes. "It's because I'm so hot, isn't it?"

He wanted to say it was because Laura was inside her somewhere, but the truth was that Vex *was* easy to stare at. Everything about her was the opposite of Laura. Tall, blonde, willowy, and conservative compared to short, dark, curvy, and dangerously sexy.

But was this the real Vex, or did the souls influence her? "I'm not staring," he lied. "I'm trying to figure you out. Do the souls affect your personality, even if they aren't trying to possess you?"

She laughed at a young Memitim who tripped over his own sword while practicing with it. "Sometimes." She turned to him, her big violet eyes still sparkling with amusement. "Like, once I killed this Alu demon asshole, and his soul got sucked into me. Do you know what they eat? Rotting flesh. Seriously. The more rotten the better. Until I was able to get rid of him, my mouth would water every time I drove past a dead animal on the side of the road." She stuck out her tongue and made a face that was so Laura-like that a wave of longing crashed over him. "So gross. And another time, I absorbed the soul of an incubus. I didn't realize it at the time, but damn, I was horny. For like, a month. Couldn't get enough, you know?"

No, he didn't know. But now he was picturing her trying to get enough, and it made him uncomfortably warm. And a little hard.

"So the souls inside you now could be influencing you?" Earlier, she'd mentioned the evil soul wanted things. Like sex.

His cock twitched, and he bit his tongue, welcoming the pain. Anything to keep from having thoughts he shouldn't be having. Laura might be influencing Vex, but it didn't matter. Vex was *not* Laura.

She shrugged. "The weaker ones might be having some minor effect, but when there's more than one, they tend to spend so much time fighting each other that they don't mess with me." She held up her hand. "Fingers crossed that SuperEvil holds to that."

Just in case, he was going to make sure Vex had a constant babysitter.

He took her to an unoccupied Motel 666 room on the second floor and sent a passing Memitim to fetch a guard. The space was small, with only the most basic of furniture, but this room had recently been vacated by an Unfallen who had given into the seduction of Sheoul, and he'd left a nice flat-screen TV behind.

She tossed her backpack to the cot. "This is it, huh? No pool? No coffee maker? No continental breakfast? I'm going to destroy you on Yelp." She jammed her fists on her hips in faux outrage, and his gaze automatically fell to the marks on her arm. "What *is* it? Why do you keep looking at them?"

He supposed it wouldn't hurt to explain why he kept staring at her and the glyphs. She was probably starting to think he was some sort of obsessive creeper.

"Because one of them is familiar," he said, his heart thumping excitedly at the reason for the familiarity. "It was something I felt when

I touched you."

She donned a wicked grin that probably got her anything she wanted from males. "Was that 'something' horny? Because if you want to touch me again, I'm okay with that." Her tone was as flirty as her smile as she dragged her fingernail over the glyphs on her arm. "So are at least two of the souls."

"No," he ground out. "That 'something' wasn't horny."

"You sure?" The sultry gleam in her eyes nearly made him groan. "Do you want to touch me again to see?"

Yes. Hell, yes. He'd kill to experience that feeling again, was desperate to connect with Laura in any way he could. And what if she could feel him, too? If he caressed Vex's smooth, tan skin, would Laura know it was his touch?

Without thinking, he reached for her, but before he made contact, Suman, a burly Memitim with more muscles than brains, jogged into the room like there was a fire.

"I was told I was needed," he said stiffly, a soldier through and through.

It was probably good that he'd shown up, because as much as Zhubaal wanted to feel Laura, he wasn't sure he wanted to experience the loss of the connection with her again.

"Thank you, Suman," Z said, snapping himself into job mode. "I need you to watch Vex for a while. I'll send someone to relieve you soon." He turned back to Vex. "There's a communal bathroom down the hall, and I'll have food sent over. Stay put." As an afterthought, he added, "And be good."

Somehow, he wasn't surprised to hear her laughter all the way out of the building, and damn if it didn't make him smile, too.

Chapter Four

Vex was going crazy. How could anyone stand being trapped in such a tiny room? She needed space. Freedom to move.

It wasn't that she wanted to escape from Sheoul-gra. She wanted to explore it. She'd just had to figure out how to get past the babysitter. First, she'd attempted to leap out of one of the glassless windows, but apparently, some sort of invisible barrier allowed for airflow but not for solid objects to pass through.

Plan B proved to be a better idea because, as it turned out, her new guard, Vane, was one of the Unfallen who lived here, and he was extremely vulnerable to seduction.

All it had taken was a little flirty chatting while she nibbled from the bowl of fruit a perky redhead named Cat had brought her. The horny bastard had been practically drooling by the time she licked juice from the second strawberry off her upper lip.

Now, as she teased him toward the bed, she pretended to untie her leggings. The moment his eager gaze focused on her hands, she kicked upward and flipped into the air, catching him under the jaw with her boot hard enough to knock him the hell out.

He hit the floor with a satisfying thud. She did feel a little bad, though. He was going to have one monster of a headache when he woke up.

After that, it was an easy walk down to the grounds, which, like everything else, was much less...well, hellish...than she'd originally expected. Surely there was more here than pristine white buildings, lush grass and palm-like trees, and a well-kept cobblestone path that led to a sparkling pond. The landscape went on and on in all directions, and she wondered about boundaries. Were there any? Or was this realm as endless as its blue-gray, featureless sky?

A dove flew overhead, startling her and once again blowing away expectations. It wouldn't have surprised her to see a raven or a vulture, or even an evisceraptor hunting for a spiny hellrat. But a dove?

She wandered down to the pond edge and propped herself against a tree trunk. The peacefulness was surreal here, in a place everyone associated with pain, death, and horror. Even the souls, who had been buzzing like bees under her skin, had settled down. Really, the Grim Reaper should be ashamed of himself. He wasn't so scary, was he? Maybe his reputation was all based on a big act, while in reality he was a big wuss. She'd encountered demons like that, who were all tough talk and very little action.

The Azagoth you met was no inferior being, and you know it.

Well, she could hope. Yes, she needed him to be willing to buy the souls inside her, but she'd also like to get out of this situation alive and with a monetary agreement that would secure her future, so if she had to fantasize that he was a big wuss, then that's what she'd do.

Heck, this entire realm was probably full of big wusses. The distant sounds of the Memitim and Unfallen in their training, mostly shouts, thuds, and screams of pain, didn't do much to back up her wishful thinking. And neither did the sound of angry, thudding footsteps coming up the trail behind her. She was busted.

And she knew without looking that it was Zhubaal.

Deep beneath Vex's breast, SuperEvil's buzz turned into a purr of delight, desire, and wickedness.

But, to be fair, when she turned around and saw Zhubaal standing there, his muscular arms folded across his broad chest, she experienced the same damned feelings, and she definitely couldn't blame her lust on any one of the souls inside her.

Except her own.

* * * *

Zhubaal glared at Vex as she stood next to the pond that, not long ago, had been filled with bubbling blood and aquatic demons and beasts, all a reflection of the evil that had consumed Azagoth. Now, thanks to his happiness with Lilliana, the pond was as clear as the crystal waters off Corfu in the Ionian Sea, its glassy surface catching the shapely reflection of Vex's perfect ass. She might not be what he'd always considered to be his "type," but he found himself admiring her more than he should, especially since Laura was basically right there with them.

Harnessing his frustration and guilt to use against Vex, he barked, "What the hell were you thinking?"

Her half-hearted, dismissive shrug didn't help his mood. "I wanted to look around. I was tired of being cooped up in that little room with nothing to do except watch the History Channel, horror movies, or reruns of *Gilligan's Island.*" She looked at him as if he was at fault for the programming choices. "That's all that's on TV. Gore fests, history I don't care about, and a goofy old comedy. What's up with that? And how do you have TV down here, anyway?"

His beloved's soul was at stake here and she was worried about TV? "Who the hell cares? I could have lost her." The very thought made his chest constrict. "Don't leave your room again, or I swear, I'll chain you in it."

"Ooh, promise?"

"Yes." And he'd enjoy doing it. He could picture himself holding her against the wall as he snapped the cuffs around her slender wrists, and his groin tightened. So...yeah, he'd enjoy it. Too much.

Snorting, Vex kicked at a stick that was half-buried in the pebbles surrounding the pond. "I'm surprised you don't have a dungeon."

"We do. Several, including the ones Hades runs in the Inner Sanctum."

"Cool," she said. "Dungeons are...wait. Hades? He's real?"

Z nodded, because Hades was real, all right. A real dick.

"Huh." She jammed her fists on her hips and glanced around the landscape. "I'm learning all kinds of new shit today." Cocking her head, she studied him. "You said you could have lost her. Lost who?"

Damn. This chick could change a subject faster than an angel could flap his wings. "No one," he ground out. "And you could have *asked* Vane to show you around instead of knocking him out. You aren't a prisoner." Well, technically, she was, since he wouldn't allow her to leave until she released Laura's spirit. Small details.

"Oh. Well, how was I supposed to know?" She bent to pick a daisy growing at the water's edge, which allowed him a stellar view of her leather-wrapped backside until he forced himself to avert his gaze. "You told me to stay put."

"And look how well that worked," he muttered.

She straightened, her nose buried in the flower. "Is Azagoth back?"

"Nope."

She frowned, nose still in the daisy, and he couldn't help but admire the juxtaposition of this heavily armed warrior woman taking pleasure in a delicate flower. "When?"

"He'll be back when he's back." Azagoth rarely gave timeframes for anything, which was especially strange because he was usually an annoyingly structured person.

"That's very helpful," she said so brightly that he almost missed the sarcasm. "Where did he go? I heard him say he was going to…what was that place you just mentioned? The Inner Sanctum? What's that?"

He didn't see any point in lying or denying her information, and besides, he didn't have anything better to do. Razr was monitoring the portal, Lilliana was managing the Unfallen, and Z had made sure the kitchens, laundry, and groundskeepers were all on track. The rest of the day was his.

"The Inner Sanctum is where the souls go after Azagoth gets done with them," he said. "Some call it Purgatory, some call it a prison, but it's really just a big holding tank."

"I wondered where all the souls were." Curiosity glinted in Vex's remarkable eyes. Laura's interest had been easily piqued, as well, and he wondered if she was listening. "So, what's it like inside the Inner Sanctum? Is it…hell? The kind humans preach about? Or is it like this?" She made an expansive gesture with her hand. "Because this isn't very terrifying."

"You didn't see Sheoul-gra back before Azagoth found a mate." He watched her slender fingers tuck the daisy behind her ear, and he was once again struck by the stark contrast of the fragile daisy against her tough exterior. It fascinated him and left him conflicted because he couldn't figure out if he was attracted to *her*...or if he was attracted to her because Laura was in there somewhere. "But the Inner Sanctum is still mostly the stuff of nightmares."

"Mostly?"

He scooped a smooth round stone off the ground and skipped it across the pond, enjoying the tiny thrill it brought. He hadn't skipped stones since his youth, when Ipsylum drill sergeants took trainees to lakes in the human realm so they could learn aquatic combat techniques where the water was denser and colder than in Heaven. He and his friends—and Laura—would have rock-skipping contests during their breaks.

She'd always won.

"There are different levels, or rings, where the demons go, depending on how inherently evil they are," he said as the tiny ripples in the water died down. "They match up with the *Ufelskala* tiers you mentioned. Level one isn't much different than life here, really." According to Azagoth, Laura had been assigned to the first level after she'd been slaughtered, but she'd been reborn before Z had a chance to find her there. "The other levels get progressively more violent and miserable."

"Ah." She nodded as if she'd come to a great realization. "So that's why."

"That's why what?"

She smiled, and he cursed how easily she stirred his blood. It was wrong to be aroused by Vex when Laura was so close. And when he couldn't do anything about it anyway. His virginity belonged to Laura and always had.

"Why you aren't a total evil asshole," she said. "I mean, you might be an asshole, I kind of think you are, but you aren't *eeeevil*. Not super evil, the way fallen angels usually are. You know what's inside the Inner Sanctum, so you're trying to stay...I dunno, decent, I guess. That way, when you meet whatever horrible end you're destined to suffer, you don't get assigned to a lower level."

Whatever horrible end he was destined to suffer? He'd bet her horrible end came before his. But otherwise, what she'd said was true. He did struggle to keep evil from darkening his soul, something that was far easier now that Azagoth and his realm weren't steeped in hatred and malevolence.

Zhubaal had suffered like everything else in Sheoul-gra while the Grim Reaper's soul grew more and more sinister and corrupt. But now that much of the darkness had been lifted, and knowing what life was like in the Inner Sanctum, Zhubaal had sworn to never let himself sink too deeply into evil temptations. The Inner Sanctum's first level was absolutely his goal.

They had beer there.

"So...you have a girlfriend?"

Once again, the change of topic gave him whiplash, but he managed to shake his head.

She picked up a rock and skipped it like he had, except her stone went farther. "Then who is the 'her' you mentioned when you were yelling at me?"

"I wasn't yelling." He looked around for another rock. He couldn't let her win. "And it's complicated."

"Hmm. Complicated, you say." She tapped her finger on her chin, and he could practically hear the wheels turning in her head as she tried to figure out what "complicated" meant. He wished her luck with that. He couldn't untangle it himself.

"So this person...are you in love with her? Is she emotionally unavailable? Or involved with someone else?" Vex sucked in a sharp breath. "Ooh, that's it, isn't it? Being involved with someone else would be really complicated. So who is she? Azagoth's mate?" She clapped her hands, delighted by the gossipy speculation. "It is!"

"It's not Lilliana, and don't even think that." He found a stone of adequate shape and size and dug it out of the ground with his fingers. "Azagoth is dangerously territorial. Once a dude leered at her for too long, and then he made this slurping noise at her..." He shook his head, still amazed by the male's stupidity and Azagoth's swift and brutal reaction.

Vex bounced on her toes like a child listening to an exciting bedtime story. "Did he kill the dude?"

"No," Z said, "but he won't be looking at Lilliana again. He won't be looking at *anyone* again."

"Azagoth seems really dreamy," she sighed, and wasn't she a bloodthirsty little thing. So opposite of Laura, but he had to admit that he found that attractive in a female. Cruelty, no, but there was nothing wrong with a little eye-for-an-eye. Or an eye for a leer. "I mean, scary, too. But dreamy."

The twinge in his gut wasn't jealousy that she was drooling over Azagoth. It wasn't. Fuck that. "You and I have a very different idea of what constitutes dreamy."

"Yeah?" She folded her arms beneath her breasts, pushing them up even more, and damn her for drawing his eyes to her bold curves. "What's your idea?"

Hmm...should he go for brutal honesty or opt for tact? "The opposite of you." Brutal honesty.

She grinned, all ruby lips and perfect white teeth. "So...hideous? And scrawny. And lacking intelligence." She swept her hand through her short violet-tipped black hair. "And blonde."

Well, she had one of those right. Laura had been as blonde as he was, but her silky mane had flowed like molten gold all the way to her waist. He'd often imagined threading his fingers through it while they made love. And when he was feeling really *randy*, as they used to say, he'd fantasized about wrapping her braid around his fist and taking her roughly, propelling her to climax after climax until they fell, exhausted, onto their marriage mattress. Not that he would ever have told her that. Laura would have been shocked. Maybe even repulsed.

Vex tweaked his nose. "Dillyoon."

He froze, as stunned by the fact that she'd just *tweaked his fucking nose* as he was by what she'd said. His mind flashed back to Laura and how she'd teased him in an identical way so long ago. "How do you know that word?"

"Dunno." She shrugged. "Just one of those things you hear, I guess. Why? What's a dillyoon?"

Azagoth, where are you? Zhubaal needed to get Laura's soul out of Vex. *Now.* Laura had to be influencing Vex's behavior, and he didn't know how much more of it he could take.

"It's a type of butterfly faerie that exists only in one small region in Heaven," he said, watching her carefully for more signs that Laura was...what? Trying to communicate with him? Was that even possible?

"Its wings are white lace, and its body is luminescent emerald. They get off on teasing angels." Laura had found them to be both adorable and annoying. He'd come down on the side of annoying.

"I met a faerie once." Vex wrinkled her nose. "They're mean."

"You've met the demonic version," he said. "Not the Heavenly one."

This time, her grin was sinister, and his body hardened, dammit. Had to be Laura. Had to be. There was no way his taste in females had changed this drastically. His dreams had always involved his lovely, virginal Laura, not leather-clad, half-naked, seductive teases.

"The demonic versions do not like flyswatters." Vex gave him a playful wink, and suddenly, it was like being in Heaven with Laura, taking a walk through the Iridescent Forest in between combat training sessions.

He moved nearer, studying her closely, as if he looked hard enough he'd see his beloved in Vex's eyes. "Is one of the spirits affecting you? Right now, I mean."

She paused, lifting her face to his until they were only inches away. "I don't know. I think...maybe. I feel more comfortable with you than I should. Isn't that odd?"

He watched her full lips as she talked, but he barely heard what she'd said. His focus narrowed on her mouth, until only one thing was on his mind.

"Shh," he murmured. "Kiss me."

"Excuse me?"

He didn't give her a chance to be outraged. He lowered his head and captured her mouth. Instant heat sizzled through him, catching him off guard. He'd only kissed one female since his fall from Heaven, and while the kiss had been arousing, it hadn't been remarkable. It had happened during a moment of weakness, when he'd nearly given up on finding Laura, and Cat had been there, needing him as much as he needed...something. But yeah, not remarkable.

This was *beyond* remarkable. It was familiar, and he could almost believe it was calling to his soul.

His body tightened as desire warmed his blood and brought an erotic, pulsing ache to his groin. Without thinking, he tugged the female against him, loving the press of her breasts into his chest. A delicate moan broke from her throat as she wrapped her leg around his thigh and rubbed her sex against the hard ridge of his cock.

"Laura," he whispered, and before her name had even faded from the air, he cringed with both guilt over kissing Vex and anger that he was letting himself get way too distracted. He was forgetting decades of discipline training that had afforded him endless endurance, patience, and even control over his bodily functions.

Pulling away, Vex scowled up at him, her eyes sparking violet fire. "Who the hell is Laura? An ex, I'm guessing?" She sucked in a sharp breath, her anger replaced by curiosity. "Ooh, is Laura also known as Ms. Complicated?"

He scrubbed his hand over his face. "You could say that." Inhaling deeply, he willed his pulse to idle out and his breathing to stop sounding as if he'd run a marathon.

"Do I remind you of her?"

For some reason, that amused him. "You are nothing like her. But you feel like her. And I haven't felt her in a long time."

She grimaced and backed away. "Ew. So you're perving all over me because my skin is as luxuriously smooth as hers or some shit? Where is she? Why haven't you seen her in a long time?"

"She was lost to me nearly a hundred years ago," he said. "She was reborn, but now...I think she's dead again."

"So she died twice? Talk about shitty luck." She narrowed her eyes at him. "Did you kill her one of those times?"

"No, and your skin isn't what I feel." Well, he had felt Vex's skin, and damned if it wasn't luxuriously smooth like she'd said. "It's what's inside you, Vex. Some of the things you're saying, the way you just kissed me." He closed his eyes, trying to hold on to the feelings the kiss had awakened, but all that did was make his pulse race again. "I think one of the souls you're carrying around is Laura."

"Oh." Out of the blue, she cupped his cock through his pants, and he somehow managed to not moan in ecstasy. "And here I thought I was the one giving you this impressive hard-on."

"It was you," he said, and for some reason, that irritated him. His brain might have been blowing circuits over Laura, but the rest of his body had been all about Vex. He stepped back, and it pissed him off that he did it reluctantly.

"Was this Laura person a succubus?"

He nearly laughed. "Hardly." At least, not in her first life. He had no idea what species she'd been during the second. "Why?"

Vex's voice went low and throaty, which made him even harder. "Because you make me wet."

"*What?*" he croaked.

Vex idly trailed her fingers through her cleavage, and his mouth was suddenly parched. "From the moment I got here, I've wanted to jump your bones. Maybe that's your girl talking."

He swallowed. Hard. "She wouldn't. Not through you. Not like that."

"You sure about that? Because right now, all I want is to drop to my knees and take you in my mouth." Before he could search his brain for a response, she went down to her knees in front of him, gripped his hips, and pressed her lips to the bulge in his jeans. The feel of her hot breath through the fabric and the bruising grip of her fingers digging into his ass cheeks froze him in place, his body completely shutting down his brain.

This is wrong.

She kissed lower on his shaft and then began to nibble her way up, following the slight curve of his cock behind the fly of his pants. Her head bobbed as she went, giving him the most erotic view he'd ever seen, and they weren't even doing anything. Not really.

If some male was kissing Laura between her legs through her pants, would they also not be doing anything?

Oh, hell, no. Raw, possessive anger expanded in his chest, and he stepped back with a hiss. Laura would never allow that to happen.

The Laura you knew wouldn't, but in her second life, she could have been a whore in Satan's harem.

Or a succubus.

"No!" he broke away, the lust so thick in his voice he nearly choked on it. "I told you. She wouldn't do this through you. She's not like you."

"No shit." Vex shoved to her feet, anger putting red splotches in her cheeks. "I'm alive and she's not."

Her words hit him like a blow, because as much as he hated to admit it, she was right. Yes, he was ninety-nine-point-nine percent sure he'd found Laura, but it wasn't as if they could be together. She would be sent to the Inner Sanctum, and even if Azagoth allowed Zhubaal to transfer to Hades's employ so he could be with her, she could be reincarnated at any moment, and he'd be in this same position all over again. Yes, he was thrilled to have found Laura, but this situation was less than ideal.

"I—" He broke off as a sharp buzz vibrated in his head.

Vex cocked her head at him, curiosity overriding anger once again. "Zhubaal? What is it?"

"It's Azagoth. He's back." And just in the nick of time.

Chapter Five

Vex wasn't sure what she expected to find inside Azagoth's office, but a relatively normal place of business wasn't it. The room was dark, decorated in blacks, grays, and mahogany, with a massive fireplace against one wall, the flames inside shooting six feet and more into the air. His monstrous claw-footed desk took up at least a fifth of the room, and as big as the desk was, the male sitting behind it made it seem small.

The souls inside her shrieked, throwing themselves against the barriers of her mind so forcefully that it felt like someone was taking a baseball bat to her skull. She furtively wiped away a bead of blood that dripped from her nose and cursed the marks on her arm that burned like fresh brands in Azagoth's presence.

But then, Zhubaal's rejection and insult burned nearly as badly.

She's not like you. She wouldn't drop to her knees to give a perfect stranger a blowjob.

Okay, he hadn't said that second part out loud, but the subtext had been as blatant as a triclops's third eye. And dammit, she could hardly believe she'd come on to him like that. Oh, she was unashamedly bold when it came to the opposite sex, but she'd never been *that* bold. The stupid souls inside her were playing some serious games with her sex drive and willpower. And thanks to this Laura person, Vex felt like she knew Zhubaal, which only ramped up her arousal and made his sexual pull even stronger.

"My Lord," Zhubaal said, and God, even his voice turned her on. It seemed like the more time she spent with him, the more time she *wanted* to spend with him. "Vex is a *daemani* with five souls on board." He glanced over at Vex's arm. "I believe one of them is Laura."

Vex watched from where she'd remained near the entrance as Azagoth's gaze cut sharply to hers, his emerald eyes glinting in the firelight. His expression was stony, forbidding, and she wondered if he ever smiled. Then she decided she didn't want to know what amused him, because if he was a typical evil maniac with godlike powers, he enjoyed pain, suffering, and death.

His gaze intensified, and she suddenly felt exposed. Vulnerable. The souls inside her shrieked louder.

He gave her a "come here" gesture with his finger. "Hello, Vex."

Trying desperately to ignore the pounding in her head, she strode all the way in, determined not to show an ounce of fear. Zhubaal remained where he was, and despite the fact that she was annoyed at him, she felt better that he stayed.

She also felt better when she caught him admiring her ass while she walked. Laura could suck it.

Clearing her throat, she stopped in front of Azagoth's desk. "Mr. Reaper."

"You can call me Azagoth." Leaning forward in his seat, he folded his hands together on his desktop. "When did you discover that you were a *daemani*?"

She had no idea why that was important, and she'd made a rule about not answering personal questions posed by massively powerful demons, but Azagoth didn't seem like the type who appreciated being dodged. So he was going to get a very personal answer.

"The day I started my period," she said, amused by the way his brow arched. Only a millimeter, but still. Zhubaal's exasperated groan was even funnier. "When I was thirteen."

Her parents had taken her to an underworld festival that day, even though she'd practically been doubled over with cramps. *Toughen up, sweetheart,* her mom had said. *If you can't handle that kind of pain, what are you going to do when some Aegis slayer runs you through with a blade?*

No Aegi had ever stabbed Vex, but at the festival, a Nightlash demon had been gutted right in front of her. She'd watched in horror as his soul rose from his dead body and got sucked inside her. No one else had seen, but when she told her parents what had happened, they'd taken her immediately to a friend of theirs, a fallen angel who was also a *daemani*. With Malice's guidance, Vex had built a business out of her ability, and she'd done well until now. Now she needed Azagoth's help to get back on her feet.

"Can you repel them?" he asked. "Or expel them without a conduit or another *daemani*?"

"No to all of it." She didn't like admitting to her weaknesses, but she suspected Azagoth would know if she was lying, and he was the last person she'd want catching her in a fib.

"And why, exactly, are you here?"

She took a deep, bracing breath. This was it, the moment that could save her livelihood...and her life. "I'm here to make you an offer."

"What kind of offer?"

"Put me on your payroll," she said firmly, "and I'll bring you souls." Man, if she could pull this off, she'd be the most infamous *emim* ever. Her parents would be so proud.

Azagoth's slow smile was so chilly she nearly shivered, and there went her dreams of infamy. "I already have people who bring me souls, and I don't have to pay them."

"Your *griminions* are only summoned when a demon dies," she pointed out. "I can bring you rogue souls that roam loose or that escape from their enclosures."

"And why should I care about them?"

"Aren't you in the *business* of souls?" She stepped closer, pressing her point home to take a position of strength. *Thank you, Daddy, for the lessons in negotiation.* She might have detested her father's lectures even more than her mother's combat training, but as a lawyer at a demon-run law firm, he'd known what he was talking about. So had her mother. "You were given an *entire realm* in order to house the spirits of those without physical bodies. It's your *job*."

His smirk said he didn't acknowledge her position of strength. And he might even be entertained by it. What a dick. "And how long did it take you to collect those five souls?"

"A couple of months," she said. "But that's only because I wasn't actively looking for them. I figure on average I can collect one rogue soul every sixteen hours."

The smirk got smirkier. "A single *griminion* can bring me a hundred in a day."

"Well, good for them," she said, her confidence flagging as she reached for the only ace she had. "But can they see rips in the fabric between dimensions? Can they capture the souls that squeeze through those rips?" She held out her arm, the glyphs glowing on her skin. "Because that's how I collected most of these."

Azagoth rose smoothly to his feet. "You can see the fissures in the walls of Sheoul-gra's Inner Sanctum?"

"Ah...I...guess?" She'd taken a stab in the dark with the dimensions thing. She hadn't known where the souls came from. "Not only can I see them, but I can sense where a rip is going to open." Usually they opened miles from where she was, and now that the market for souls had dried up, she'd gotten into the habit of going in the opposite direction to avoid picking up an evil hijacker. But sometimes, like yesterday, they popped open right in front of her.

Zhubaal eyed her speculatively. "I assume you usually sell the souls." He clenched his jaw, and she could only assume that he'd just realized that his precious Laura could have been sold to a slaver or soul-eater. "So why are you here instead of hashing out a deal in some skeezy necromancer's lair?"

"I *was* in some skeezy necromancer's lair. He told me to come to Azagoth." Zhubaal got that judgey look on his face again, and she huffed. "The market vanished almost overnight. Buyers and sellers are either dying or disappearing. The few buyers who are still around refuse to see me or anyone else hawking souls."

Other *daemani* were talking about forming a union and demanding answers. From whom, Vex had no idea. And given that someone was killing *daemani*, gathering together in a group didn't seem like the best plan ever.

Azagoth passed his hand through the flames in the fireplace, but they didn't burn him. In fact, the flames parted, as if terrified to so much as warm his skin. "So what you're saying is that you're so desperate to get rid of those souls that you are willing to risk your own soul by coming to me. Is that about right?"

Something about the cool, calm way he spoke made her internal alarms go off, and she got the sudden feeling she was walking into a trap. Her father would have told her to stay calm. Her mother would have told her to get ready for a fight.

Her mother hadn't possessed an ounce of self-preservation instinct.

"Yes," she said, going with her father's line of thinking, "but without the desperate part. I'm not desperate." She was *so* desperate. "And I'd rather not risk my soul. Zhubaal told me about the Inner Sanctum. No, thank you." She bounced on her toes and crossed her fingers behind her back in a ridiculous superstitious human gesture. "So we have a deal?"

Azagoth smiled, and a chill went down her spine. "The deal is this. You are going to hunt for souls, but I'm not going to pay you."

Before she knew it, she had a blade in her palm and was starting toward him. *Oh, hi, Mom.* "What the hell? What kind of bullshit is that?"

Zhubaal's hand clamped down on her shoulder, and he yanked her backward, disarming her so quickly she stared at her empty hand in disbelief.

Azagoth didn't miss a beat, and it was a little insulting that he didn't think she was enough of a threat to even waste an angry tone of voice on. "You need someone to dump the souls on, and there are very few people left who are willing to risk the King of Hell's wrath." Her expression must have been one of surprise, because he snorted. "What, you think I don't have my finger on the pulse of the underworld? You think I don't know that *daemani* are being hunted at the command of the king himself?" He laughed, but she certainly didn't find this to be funny in the least. "Foolish girl. I don't need you as much as you need me."

Son. Of. A. Bitch.

"I have to eat, you know." She snatched the dagger from Zhubaal and jerked out of his grip. Which was nothing like the way he'd gripped her earlier, his hands pressed firmly against her hip and the small of her back. "Selling souls is how I make a living."

Well, it used to be, back when buying and selling was a thriving market. She'd made a lot of money, but she'd lost it all when the underworld and human stock markets crashed during the recent near-apocalypse. Everything was gone now. Even her Audi and her two-million-dollar condo in sunny Florida were going to be repossessed soon.

Maybe she should have gone to college like her parents wanted instead of pursuing a career in trading souls. But come on, it was easy money, and she'd earned far more than she'd ever have made with any college career. They'd understood, but they hadn't liked it.

Azagoth folded his hands behind his back and faced her squarely. "If you want to be paid, then I expect daily results. I don't want five souls every three months, and I'm not going to pay per soul. You can move into one of the town residences if you need a place to stay. You will bring at least one escapee per day, and your salary will be no more than Zhubaal's."

She glanced over at Zhubaal, who shrugged apologetically. "Look at the bright side," he said. "You'll be too busy to need money, anyway."

Shit. She was trapped, and there was no way out of it. Azagoth might be a penny-pinching miser, but he was going to keep her safe. Plus, she got to brag to everyone that she worked with the Grim Reaper.

"Fine," she muttered. "It's a deal. Can we get these souls out of me now?"

Azagoth turned to Zhubaal. "Leave us."

Zhubaal went taut, his gaze shifting between Vex and Azagoth. "No, my Lord, I think I'll stay."

The temperature in the room dropped so fast she saw Azagoth's breath in the air when he spoke next. "I didn't give you a choice."

Baring his fangs, Zhubaal put himself between her and Azagoth. "I have been searching for Laura for nearly a hundred years," he said, his voice walking a fine line between respect and defiance, "and now that I've finally found her, I won't let anything happen to her."

Vex peeked around Zhubaal's shoulder and instantly wished she hadn't. Azagoth was pissed. She'd never seen eyes of flame before, and she never wanted to again. Holy crap, Zhubaal had some serious stones.

"Vex." If Azagoth's eyes were the fire, his voice was the black smoke. "Wait outside my office."

No. He'll kill Zhubaal.

Vex shook her head, trying to rid it of Laura's influence. And those thoughts *had* to be Laura's, because Vex didn't give a shit about the guy. Sure, he had some major appeal; he was hot as hell, probably knew his way around a bedroom, and he had giant balls...both real and figuratively. She knew because she'd gotten in a good fondle earlier by the pond, before he'd freaked out because she wasn't his stupid Laura.

She's not like you.

Right. Laura would probably stay and defend her adoring Zhubaal. So Vex left him on his own.

* * * *

Zhubaal had probably made his last mistake, but right now he couldn't care less. Every instinct inside him demanded that he protect Laura, and if he had to give up his soul to do it, he would. She'd looked so desperate standing there, just as Azagoth had said.

That was Vex. Not Laura.

Damn it, he hated that the lines kept blurring with Vex, but it wouldn't be that way for much longer. Azagoth would free Laura and separate the two.

Zhubaal just might not be alive to see it.

"What the fuck was that?" Azagoth rounded on Zhubaal the moment Vex was out of the room. His eyes were pure flame, hot enough to scorch Z's face. "You have never disobeyed an order."

The fact that Z wasn't already dead was a good sign. "I never had reason not to."

"You still don't," he growled. "What the fuck did you think I was going to do to Laura?"

Anger over decades of Azagoth's vague answers and flat-out refusals to answer questions boiled over, and Z lost his shit. His wings sprouted, his fangs punched down, and he drew every ounce of power Azagoth allowed into his body.

"I don't know what you're going to do," Zhubaal snarled. "Maybe send Laura to the Inner Sanctum before I can see her? Or maybe reincarnate her so I have to go through another thirty years of hell looking for her?"

The flames in Azagoth's eyes snuffed out as he held up his hand, genuine confusion in his expression. "Why would you think I'd do that?"

"You tell me. Why did you keep Laura from me all this time? Why didn't you tell me anything about her identity? I could have found her. Saved her before she was killed and ended up as a welt on Vex's body."

Azagoth shook his head. "I didn't know anything about her."

Z gaped at him in disbelief. "How could you not know? You're the Grim Reaper. Souls are your *job*," he said, echoing Vex from just a moment ago.

"I authorize a specific number of souls from each level to be reincarnated every day, but after the individuals are chosen, they enter the Infernal Abyss to be cast into a waiting fetus. Who—and what—they are born as is out of my hands or realm of knowledge."

Son of a bitch. "You couldn't have told me this earlier?"

"Would this information have helped you locate Laura?"

"No, but—"

"Then drop it." Azagoth's tone was deceptively mild, which meant he was reaching the end of civility. Which, Z could admit, had gone on much longer than he'd expected.

"At least tell me why you wanted me to leave the room while you extracted the souls from Vex."

Azagoth tapped a glass pad on the wall behind his desk, and a panel slid back, revealing a well-stocked bar, the newest upgrade to his office. "Because you don't need to see what I'm going to do to her." He poured vodka in two glasses and brought one to Z.

Baffled, he took the glass. "I'm not squeamish."

And he wasn't. He'd done things as an angel that had made his buddies puke for hours afterward, and he'd done worse as a fallen angel. But even as the words fell from his mouth, he doubted them. Vex shouldn't matter to him, but he didn't want to see her hurt. She'd brought Laura to him, and that had, at the very least, earned her his eternal gratitude.

"I know." Azagoth downed the liquor, and as he lowered the glass, shadows darkened his eyes. "But there are some things loved ones should never see."

It took a moment to let Azagoth's words sink in, and when they did, Zhubaal was glad he had the alcohol.

Holy crap. Azagoth was protecting him. Zhubaal had seen Laura's remains, her chest cavity laid open and her heart removed. The nightmares still haunted him, and Azagoth knew it, thanks to his love of throwing massive annual celebrations for Sheoul-gra's residents who had survived since the last party. At the most recent event, Zhubaal had had one too many of Azagoth's signature cocktails, a Bloody Reaper, and he'd blubbered all about his bad dreams. The next day, Azagoth hadn't said a word about it.

But he *had* poured Z another Bloody Reaper, because apparently, Z had looked like he'd needed "a little hair of the hellhound."

"I still want to be there when you free the souls," Zhubaal said. "If it were Lilliana, wouldn't you want to be there?"

"Fuck, yeah," Azagoth said. "And no one could tell me no. But it would be a mistake." He clapped his hand on Z's shoulder. "Trust me, Z. You don't want to see it, and I can't have you interrupting. There's a powerful soul inside Vex that could put up a fight, and I'm going to need all my focus to draw it out."

Z got that. During battle, even the most minor distraction could be deadly. Azagoth wouldn't be in any danger, but Vex could be. And if Azagoth had to destroy the evil soul inside Vex, the other souls could get caught in friendly fire. It wouldn't be the first time Zhubaal had seen it happen.

"Fine," Z agreed reluctantly. "I'll send in Vex. But I'll be right outside the door."

He didn't wait for Azagoth's response. He put down his glass and stepped into the hallway where Vex was waiting, lounging back against a pillar, one foot propped against the stone behind her.

"Took you long enough." She popped away from the wall. "Is he ready?"

He gestured to the door. "Go on in."

She started to go, but paused after a couple of steps. "You're not coming in, are you?"

The way she said it, her voice an impossible mix of hope and disappointment, made his gut twinge. He liked her. She might drive him insane, but there was something about her that made him want to learn more about her. He wished he could blame his desire on any influence Laura might be having on her, but it wasn't true. It was Vex's spiky hair he wanted to touch. It was Vex's lips he wanted to kiss. It was Vex's body he wanted beneath him.

"No," he croaked.

"'Kay." Abruptly, she spun around and kissed him. She tasted like rainwater and flowers, reminding him of the pond and how good she'd felt against him. Just as abruptly, she bounced back with a cheeky smile. "Wish me luck."

With that, she disappeared into Azagoth's office while Zhubaal stood there, his excitement to see Laura tempered by his worry for Vex.

Chapter Six

Vex had no idea why she'd just kissed Zhubaal as if they were a real couple and she was seeking a good luck kiss before a job interview.

Wish me luck!

Ugh. She was an idiot. An idiot who was about to reunite him with the love of his life. And, apparently, afterlife.

Mentally cursing herself, she strode across the floor to where Azagoth was waiting expectantly by the fire. He watched her approach, and the closer she got, the more the room closed in on her. It had seemed so big before, but now it felt like a bathroom stall at McDonald's.

"I'm not sure how this will go," he said. "But we'll try the easy way first."

Oh, yes, she was all for the easy way. She'd gone through this a bazillion times, and everyone had a different method—most were quick and painless. But then, the souls she was selling always wanted to be freed, probably because they didn't know they were going to be captured by someone else. This current batch of souls knew, and they were already starting to claw at her mind.

Azagoth stepped up to her, stopping mere inches away. She expected him to start chanting like the warlocks, mages, and sorcerers she usually dealt with. Or that maybe he'd mix a potion or slice her palm and make her stand inside a protective circle while she bled on the symbols. Instead, he simply placed his hand on her forehead.

The souls went ballistic. Pain shot through her, a searing, mind-bending agony that felt like someone was pulling her spinal cord out of the top of her head.

"Stop," she gasped. "They don't want out."

"Of course they don't." He stepped back and the pain melted away, leaving behind a faint headache and wobbly knees. But the souls, stunned as far as she could tell, had quieted down to almost total silence. "Inside you, they feel safe. But they can sense me, and they know what I am. They know where they are because all but one have been here before." Shadows seemed to writhe in his eyes, and for a split second, she swore she saw a demonic face looking at her from behind his handsome one. "They know I judge harshly, they know Hades is waiting for them, and they know I'm going to send them to him."

Usually when demons said they were going to send you to Hades, they were being all blowhardy. But Azagoth sold it and made it fresh. Really fresh. She was about to pee in her favorite leather pants.

"Okay, I get why they're resisting, but you're the Grim Reaper." Did she really have to point this out? "You deal in souls. Shouldn't you, of all people, be able to suck some souls out of someone?"

"Yes." He looked troubled, which could only be bad. Really, really bad. "I should be able to extract the weaker ones without even trying."

"Then what's going on?"

Crimson glints flashed in his eyes, burning like angry embers, and she wondered if the flamethrower eyes would come next. She took a step back, just in case. "The powerful soul is holding them back. *They* want out."

"What?" She looked down at the marks on her arm as if the newest glyph could provide answers, but it wasn't any different than the others. It hadn't grown horns or teeth or formed demonic symbols. "The thing inside me is so bad that they'd rather deal with *you*?"

"I'm not sure if that's a compliment or not," he said dryly. "But in any case, the evil inside you is ancient. Perhaps as old as I am. It's going to take more than my command for her to leave your body."

Her? "I knew it!"

"Knew what?"

"That the super evil soul was female. Females claw more than males." Males were more about the blunt force trauma.

"I see." Azagoth clearly didn't care. He raked her with his gaze. "Now, take off your clothes."

"If this is some kind of bullshit ploy to get me to have sex with you—"

"I have a mate." His eyes glowed orange now, as if they were sucking the colors out of the fire, and the blood in her veins froze. And at the same time, a stab of envy pierced her because Azagoth's mate was lucky to have a male who was so fiercely faithful.

"Okay then," she said brightly, because awkward.

It took only a minute to strip down, and then she stood there, shivering even though she wasn't cold, as she waited for whatever he was going to do. She'd never been shy or self-conscious about her body, but there was something unsettling about being naked in front of someone who could probably see all the way to her soul.

As he moved toward her, he unbuttoned his shirt. "This is going to hurt." For the first time, there was a touch of sympathy in his voice. Which couldn't be a good thing. But neither could the fact that he'd just tossed his shirt onto the desk and was reaching for his belt.

What was he doing? "Will it hurt bad?"

"That depends." He stopped a foot away and peeled off his pants.

He was a commando guy, and holy shit, he was beautiful. It made her want to see Zhubaal like that, to see the six-pack she'd felt under his shirt and the erection she'd caressed with her lips. But this wasn't Zhubaal, so she snapped her gaze up to his face and locked it there.

"Depends on what?" she croaked in a humiliatingly rough voice.

"On whether you think agony is bad."

She nodded. "I do."

He laughed.

And then he punched his hand through her rib cage. Searing, ripping agony exploded through her entire body. The souls screeched and tore at her from the inside. The pain became all-consuming, the smell of blood made her gag, and she swore Azagoth's hand was wrapped around her spine.

She screamed as he yanked a bloody, squirming mass from her and threw it to the floor. Through her haze of pain, she managed a gasp of surprise. The thing writhing a few feet away was one of the demons that had been inside her, but it was in solid form. She'd never seen them as anything but ghostly wisps. Most of the time she couldn't even make out their species.

But the thing moaning on the floor was a female Umber demon nearly twice her size.

A two-foot tall creature in a brown hooded robe skittered into the room from out of nowhere, snatched up the bloody demon, and chained it to the wall. A *griminion*, she thought, and then she was immersed again in pain as Azagoth smashed his fist inside her body.

Twice more she went through the agony, but on the fourth try, she thought she was going to die. The room spun and turned into swirls of red and black and gray, and sharp, sharp teeth. She thought the teeth belonged to Azagoth, but he didn't look like a big, horned, dragon-demon. Right?

Delirious. She was delirious, wracked with fever and broken bones.

"Fuck...hold on...fuuuuck!"

Was that Azagoth's voice? She could barely hear, could only feel pain.

At some point, she realized she was lying on her back, and she thought her eyes were open, but everything was dark. No, there was a face... handsome... smiling... Zhubaal?

It didn't feel real, more like a memory. And as the darkness took her, all she could think was that if she had to die, dying with Zhubaal might not be that bad.

* * * *

Zhubaal was used to hearing sounds of agony coming from inside Azagoth's office. He'd learned to tune it out. But this was different. He felt Vex's raw, heart-wrenching screams all the way to his marrow. Azagoth had told him to stay out, but every cell in his body demanded that he do something besides stand in a dark hallway while his female was suffering.

Except Vex wasn't his female. Laura was.

She screamed again, and after what seemed like hours but was probably a couple of minutes, he hit his limit.

Heart racing in a panicked, spastic rhythm, he threw open the door. Instantly, the door ripped out of his hand and tore off its hinges, caught up in a whirlwind of evil spinning around the office like a tornado, with Azagoth and Vex at the center. The air pressure increased a hundredfold, becoming a crushing entity that sucked the air from Z's lungs and turned his eardrums into throbbing instruments of pain.

"Azagoth," he croaked, trying to see through the wall of malevolent wind. Long, skeletal hands reached for him and demonic faces snarled at him as they flew by the doorway, only to be stretched into more streams of spinning evil. "Azagoth, *stop!*"

Azagoth, morphed into a demon twice his usual size with massive horns jutting out of his dragon-like head, stood over Vex's unconscious, naked body. His gore-coated fist clenched the throat of a male Bedim demon whose dark skin had paled with terror. Azagoth's great head swiveled around to Zhubaal. He bared his teeth and snarled, but the wind died down.

Zhubaal had seen him like this before, his inner demon released by anger or contact with pure evil. Usually it was wise to leave him alone and let him come down by himself. Even Lilliana would sometimes back out of a room if he'd taken his demon out to play.

Zhubaal wasn't backing out.

In a blur of motion, Azagoth hurled the demon to the floor where two waiting *griminions* shackled him and dragged him over to where two females, a gray-skinned Umber and a big-eyed Daeva, stood against the wall.

He stared, desperate for clues, any sense that one of those demons was Laura. Would she recognize him? Would she remember that before she was a demon, she'd been an angel?

A moan pulled his gaze back to Azagoth and Vex. His heart shot into his throat now that he could see her clearly, her body lying limp in a pool of blood. Her sternum had been torn open, ribs and mangled flesh spilling out of her chest cavity.

Memories of finding Laura's body flashed through his mind, and he broke out in a cold sweat. Her killers had left her on the floor of the shitty apartment she'd rented in Poland where, as an Unfallen, she'd tried to fit in with humans and avoid fallen angels who would try to drag her into Sheoul.

They'd killed her instead. He'd hunted them for decades, and when he'd caught them, he'd gone full-bore eye-for-an-eye on the bastards. But he couldn't forget finding Laura lying in a dried pool of blood, her chest laid open like Vex's.

Even though he knew Vex's injury was of more a psychic nature than a physical one, and even though it was already stitching itself together, all he could see was Laura lying there.

He ran toward her as Azagoth shifted into his normal form, sans clothes and splashed in blood.

"She'll be fine." Azagoth stepped away from her, leaving bloody footprints on the stone floor. He was careful to avoid stepping on his favorite Slogthu-crafted rug, though. "She's stronger than I expected."

Z dropped to his knees next to Vex, more shaken than he'd like and unsure why Azagoth would have expected anything other than strength from her. "And the souls?"

Azagoth jerked his head toward the demons. "I was only able to extract three." His voice lowered to a deadly rumble. "The bitch inside Vex is holding onto the weaker soul and I can't do anything about it. She's taunting me."

"What the hell are you talking about?" Zhubaal took Vex's hand the way he'd done with Laura. It was cold. Not two-days-dead cold, but still, too cold. "Why can't you get them out?"

"I can," he growled, anger at his failure putting an edge on his words, "but doing so will probably kill Vex."

"No." He leaped to his feet, rounding on Azagoth as if the male was going to start ripping the two remaining souls from Vex right now. "No," he said, more calmly. Why was he getting so worked up about this, anyway? "We'll find another way." He swallowed dryly and looked between the demons chained to the wall and Vex. "Where is Laura?"

"She's inside Vex."

Well, that explained why he'd been acting like a possessive idiot when it came to Vex. Closing his eyes, Zhubaal let out a nasty curse. "She's still in there with the fucking evil spirit."

A troubled look darkened Azagoth's already black expression. "Take Vex to her room until I decide what to do. And don't leave her alone. The other souls had a restraining effect on the malevolent spirit.

With little to hold it back, it could have a powerful influence on her. It could even possess her if she isn't strong enough to resist."

Cursing again, he gathered Vex's limp body in his arms and headed for the door. At the threshold he paused. "What kind of demon is this powerful soul, by the way?"

Azagoth, still naked, strode over to the bar and poured a whiskey. "When she lived in the demon realm, she was a succubus."

Z looked down at Vex, her beautiful face surprisingly peaceful in sleep, and he groaned. She'd mentioned that she thought one of the souls was a sex demon, and it turned out that she was right. Bad enough to be stuck with an attractive female, but one who could be possessed by a succubus? Throw Laura into the mix, and he was in for an impossible exercise in self-control.

Chapter Seven

Vex groaned as light pierced the barely open slits of her eyelids. Where was she? She blinked, and gradually, the blur in her vision cleared. She was in her Motel 666 room, lying on the bed with nothing covering her but a blanket. Zhubaal was sitting in the wooden chair across from her bed, his face buried in a book.

He peeked at her from over the top of the book. "Hey."

"Hey." God, she sounded like she'd swallowed a frog. "What happened?" All she could remember was pain like she'd never felt before. It was as if someone had been ripping organs from her body. She could still hear the screams, but she didn't know if they belonged to her or to the spirits as they'd been wrenched from her body.

"Azagoth removed three of the souls. You passed out, so I brought you here and cleaned you up. Lilliana and I have been taking turns staying with you since." Zhubaal twisted around and took a cup from the table beside him.

He held it out to her, and she sat up, wincing at the dull ache in her chest. Azagoth had the power of a locomotive behind his punches, didn't he?

Gingerly, she wrapped the blanket around her and took the drink from him. The greasy yellow liquid looked like chicken broth but smelled of sweet herbs. Something told her it was going to be *nasty*. But then, demonic potions were rarely made of tequila and margarita mix or milk and cocoa.

"I'm afraid to ask," she said as she eyed some floating mystery blobs, "but what is it?"

He hesitated, as if choosing his words carefully, which probably meant there was scary shit in the drink he didn't want to go into detail about. "It's a potion exorcists use to weaken souls when they've possessed someone."

"But I'm not possessed." Not yet, anyway.

"No, but Azagoth thinks it'll help prevent it from happening. Or at least make it easier for you to fight." He stretched his long legs out and crossed them at his ankles. He'd changed clothes since the last time she'd seen him, outfitted in combat boots, black military pants, and a form-fitting T-shirt. It was a good look for him, as if he was meant to be a warrior. "I consulted with a shaman physician at Underworld General to make sure it would be safe for *emim*."

Surprised winged through her at that. "Why? If it killed me, wouldn't all your problems be solved? The two remaining souls would be released." Actually, her spirit would as well. Not cool. The Inner Sanctum didn't sound all that great, and she had no desire to be reborn as an imp or a troll or some crap.

Some emotion she couldn't name softened the harsh planes of his face, but not his voice, which held the powerful tone of someone speaking an oath. "I did it because you brought Laura back to me. What you endured in Azagoth's office makes you worthy of that, at least." He gestured to the cup. "Drink it. If you don't, and the soul possesses you, death might be the next option."

Yeah...no. She glanced at the cup of hot liquid. "You're sure this will help?"

He shrugged. "Can't hurt."

"How reassuring," she said flatly. Bracing herself with a deep breath, she gulped the entire contents of the cup, and holy damn, she had to force that shit to stay down. She couldn't decide which was worse—the slimy texture, the chewy globs, or the flavor, an unholy mix of liver, rancid fat, and cinnamon with a dollop of honey.

"How long have I been out?" she rasped when she finally stopped gagging and swallowing bile.

"Twenty-one hours."

"Wow." She breathed deeply, enjoying the sensation of quiet

inside her. She could still feel the two souls, but with three others gone, there was less buzzing in her body. "I feel so much better. I mean, I'm tired, but the cacophony of souls is gone."

"Can you feel the two that are left?"

As if in answer, an oil slick of evil spread across the surface of her own soul, and with it came a wave of sexual need so powerful she nearly groaned. Closing her eyes, she inhaled slowly, concentrating on forcing the soul back into its corner. Gradually, it retreated, but it left behind the throbbing ache of arousal.

She popped open her eyes. "Nope. Don't feel a thing." Except the driving need to get him into bed. "The mincemeat tea must be helping." She stood, pulling the blanket with her. "So what now?"

He sat forward, bracing his forearms on his spread knees. "Now we figure out how to get those souls out of you."

"Why couldn't Azagoth do it?" She put aside the cup and hoped she didn't have to drink any more of the nasty stuff.

"He could, but not without killing you."

"Oh. Well, I approve of his reluctance to kill me." She bent over to gather a spare set of clothes from her pack, and the blanket fell open in the back, exposing her to the cool air and Zhubaal's eyes. She could feel his gaze on her skin, hot and hungry. But it wasn't for her, was it? She'd bet her favorite blade that Laura was one of the two souls inside her. Turning back to him, she dropped the blanket. She'd never been modest and besides, if he cleaned her up after Azagoth's gore-fest of an exorcism, he'd seen her naked already. "What about Laura?"

Hastily, he glanced away, his gaze plummeting to the woven rug beneath her feet. How could anyone who'd spent any time at all in Sheoul be so embarrassed by nudity?

"She, ah...she's still inside you."

Bingo. She pulled on a pair of silky black underwear and her favorite pleated black and blue plaid miniskirt, and Zhubaal still didn't look up. There was something very sweet and respectful about that, something she had never, ever expected to find in a fallen angel. Usually they were horndogs who'd perfected leering.

Laura, you suck.

She cleared her throat of her bitterness. It was stupid to be jealous when Zhubaal was clearly dedicated to someone else. Even if that someone else was basically a ghost.

"So, let's say Azagoth gets her out," she mused. "You can't be together anyway because she's kind of dead, right?"

"Not...exactly." His gaze flickered over to her and back to the floor when he saw she still hadn't put on her shirt. "In the Inner Sanctum and some parts of Sheoul-gra, souls are solid."

Yeah, she'd figured that last part out when the first soul Azagoth ripped out of her went from a transparent wisp to a big, ugly Umber demon.

"How long have you been searching for her?" She shrugged into a silky blue, sleeveless top that hung almost to the skirt's hem and would conceal her dagger sheathes once she was armed. As she reached next to Zhubaal for her boots, her arm brushed his leg, and she bit back a needy groan at the sexual current that sizzled through her. She shot him a furtive glance as she sank down on the mattress, but if he felt anything at all, it didn't show.

"I've been looking for her since she was kicked out of Heaven nearly a century ago." He was still lounging like he belonged in her bedroom, and dammit, why did she have to like it? "She was killed soon after and reborn thirty years ago, but I don't know what species."

"Wow, so she could have been born something gross, like a Cruentus." She shoved her foot into a boot. "What would you have done if you found her and she was something horrible?"

He crossed his thick arms over his chest, and her mouth watered at the way his muscles flexed under his tan skin. "She wouldn't be."

Saint Laura strikes again. "Oh, and you just know that." There was no way he could miss the sarcasm, and sure enough, he smirked.

"Yep."

She zipped up her boot. "I know angels have a reputation for being faithful, but aren't you taking it a bit far? What kind of angel were you, anyway?"

"I was an Ipsylum."

"A what?" She tugged on the second boot.

"Ipsylum." His gaze dropped to her boot, and she zipped it up slowly, teasingly, loving how his eyes tracked her hand. He might not be hers, but she could do her best to make him regret that. "They're a specialized class of warrior angels."

"Bullshit."

His gaze snapped up. "Bullshit?"

"Yeah. Bullshit." After her parents died at the hands of angels, she'd learned everything she could about them. "I studied all the classes of angels, and Ipsylum isn't one of them." She ticked off her fingers. "There are Cherubim, Dominions, Principalities, Thrones, Seraphim, Archangels—"

"Whatever sources you got your information from are wrong. Over thousands of years, humans gradually learned of several Orders of angels, but they don't know all of them. Didn't your parents tell you about angels?"

She shook her head as she reached for the pile of weapons lying on top of the clothes someone had brought from Azagoth's office. "They answered my questions, but they didn't offer information. I think they were ashamed by whatever it was that got them booted, you know?"

Vex strapped a tiny, thin blade to the inside of her thigh, getting a kick out of Zhubaal's furtive glances as her skirt hiked high. When she finished, she tucked her leg beneath her and sat back against the hard pillow. It wasn't as if she had anywhere else to be, so she might as well get comfortable. Besides, she liked talking to Zhubaal. He was probably only humoring her because she was Laura's genie bottle, but it had been such a long time since she'd talked to anyone on a personal level that this was kind of...refreshing.

"I think that's why we lived in the human realm instead of in Sheoul, and why my parents pretended to be human. Partly because they were ashamed." She closed her eyes at the memory of her parents telling her how much danger they were in in the human realm, hated by both fallen angels who believed they should be serving Sheoul's interests, and angels, who were just assholes. "And partly to protect me from the paranormal world."

And it had worked until she hit puberty and sucked in her first soul. When her parents sought answers, it had put them on the radar for a lot of enemies. Eventually, the enemies had caught up with them, and they'd been killed. She hadn't even been close enough to catch their souls before *griminions* had, and worse, she'd never been able to take revenge.

Her parents' killers had been angels, powerful and far beyond her reach.

"So," she said, changing the subject before she got all sappy or started crying or some shit. "What do Ipsylum do? You said they're warriors?"

He nodded. "Highly trained, very powerful. In some ways, they're more powerful than Archangels. If angels are Heaven's army, then Ipsylum are the army's special ops team."

"Huh." She idly ran her fingers down the stiletto heel of one boot to test the sharp edge of the spikes that could punch through metal, bone, and flesh during a fight. Her mother's design. "What does Heaven need with a special ops team?"

Zhubaal came to his feet in a graceful surge and moved to the glassless window next to her bed. A breeze ruffled his hair as he looked out over the courtyard.

"Heaven needs specialized soldiers to assassinate powerful demons, spy in areas of Sheoul where not even Archangels can go, rescue human or angel hostages from demons...shit like that." He clenched his hands at his sides, and she wondered if he regretted his choice to leave his angelic life.

"That's awesome." Why couldn't she have been born an angel instead of an *emim* with useless powers like attracting souls like flypaper or being able to walk in stiletto heels on any surface without ever loosing her balance? Sure, she had killer reflexes and was stronger than your average human or demon, but still, in a world where angels could fly and demons could shapeshift or become invisible or manipulate the weather, she had to stretch to be considered even average. "If I were an angel, I'd want to be one of those."

He snorted. "Somehow, I'm not surprised."

"Why?"

Frowning, he glanced down at her arm and the remaining two glyphs. "Because you're the polar opposite of Laura."

"What does she have to do with it?"

"Laura was also an Ipsylum."

"No," she blurted, seriously thrown by that. The way he'd spoken of this Laura person made her sound like a milquetoast. "Really?"

"Really." There was a tap at the door, and he answered it,

thanking whoever was on the other side for a plate piled with sandwiches and fruit. He brought it over to her and placed it on the mattress beside her. "Eat. I have a feeling we're going on a little trip soon."

"A trip?" She perked up. She loved to travel. She just never had anyone to travel with. "To where?"

"To see a wizard in Los Angeles."

"I like L.A. Not so much wizards." Vex poked at one of the sandwiches. Looked like some sort of lunchmeat and cheese on wheat, but she'd seen what passed as meat in Sheoul. "I wanted to be an actress when I was growing up. My mom said I couldn't because I wasn't human, but my dad said that half the people in Hollywood are demons anyway, so I shouldn't give up." She plucked a grape off the plate. The fruit looked safe enough.

"So why did you give up?"

"Who says I did?" She tossed the grape into the air and caught it between her teeth.

"Well," Zhubaal drawled, "I don't see Channing Tatum down here making deals with Azagoth to sell souls to make money."

Smartass. She popped the grape and chewed, buying some time while she decided whether or not she should fuck with him.

Yeah, she should.

"I haven't hit it big yet." She plucked another grape from the plate and grinned. "But I'm finding that the porn industry is a great place to start. Maybe you've seen me in something recently?"

She couldn't tell if his expression was one of judgment, disgust, or curiosity. "Ah, no."

"You're missing out," she purred. "I have an idea. Why don't you bend over, and I'll pull that stick out of your ass." She winked. "We can make it fun. With a little lube—"

"We aren't starring in one of your pornos."

He seemed more than a little irritated, which cracked her up. "What's the matter? Are you lacking an adventurous spirit?" When he didn't answer, and in fact, looked a little flustered, she took advantage, coming smoothly to her feet to face him. "Are you Mr. Missionary Only?" She moved toward him, noting how his eyes shot wide, his nostrils flared, and his breaths came faster the closer she got. "Or are you into some kind of secret kink?"

He stood his ground, tensing and widening his stance, as if he expected a battle. "You are out of line."

"Why?"

"Because I'm not...available."

She halted in front of him and reached out to drag one finger playfully down his chest. "Oh, come on. You can't tell me you've been celibate for nearly a century." His only reaction was a twitch in his cheek, but it was enough. "Seriously? You haven't been with anyone since Laura died?"

"I swore an oath to her."

Holy shit. "But she died. Twice."

"Our oaths weren't meant to be broken by death," he said gravely.

What the hell? "So you're trying to tell me that even though she was reincarnated, you expected her to somehow remember an oath she took in a past life? Do you really believe that while she was alive the second time, she was celibate, as well?"

"Yes."

She laughed. Like, full-on belly laugh. Zhubaal was either naive or delusional. Maybe both. Poor, poor male.

"Some part of her would know," he insisted, irritation making his words fall like stones. "She might not remember me or our oath, but I'm sure she would have felt that she needed to wait for the right person. Had she not died, I'd have found her, and I would have been that right person." He glanced at the two remaining glyphs on Vex's arm. "Turns out, she found me."

Seriously delusional. "You think she somehow knew I'd end up in Sheoul-gra, so she hitched a ride here with me, just to see you?"

"Stranger things have happened."

That much was true. But God, he looked so sure, and yet, so sad. Vex, who had never been in love, who had never loved anyone except her parents, felt her heart break a little for him. Zhubaal might be delusional, but he felt deeply, and he was hurting.

Vex didn't have a lot of experience comforting people, but in this, she knew she could help. More importantly, she wanted to help. Zhubaal had taken care of her and kept her safe even though he didn't have to, and it was time to pay him back.

Reaching up, she cupped his cheek, following him when he tried to turn away from her touch. "Do you want to feel her?"

"What?"

Heart pounding, she stepped into him until her breasts were pressing into the hard planes of his chest. "Use me. Feel her." She lifted her face to his. "Kiss me."

He scowled down at her, wariness flickering in his eyes. "Why would you do this?"

"Because you and Azagoth are helping me." *And because I really want to kiss you.* Yes, she wanted to help, but she wasn't completely selfless. She wanted to feel his body, his mouth, against hers. "Let me return the favor."

For a long moment, he hesitated, his gaze locked on hers. Then, slowly, he dipped his head and captured her mouth with tentative pressure. The kiss was light, unsure, but she felt the sizzle all the way to her soul.

He wants Laura.

Of course he does. That's what this was about. Laura.

His tongue flicked across her lips, and she opened for him, inviting him into a deeper connection. Their tongues met, tangling together as he hauled her hard against him. Everything in her body lit up like fireworks, as if this was meant to be.

It's Laura. She must have sensed him, because all of a sudden, Vex's heart was beating in a spastic rhythm that didn't make sense. And then, as her heart beat even faster, practically throwing itself against her rib cage as if it wanted to break out and get to him, the reality hit her.

Her heart was beating for *him.*

A vague sense of love and need and loyalty wrapped around her like a warm blanket. It felt so foreign, yet so good and right. She'd never experienced anything like this, and her first thought was that her life had been so empty.

But this wonderful sensation didn't belong to her, did it? It belonged to the spirit inside her who she was beginning to hate. Zhubaal's precious Laura didn't even have a physical form, and yet she commanded fierce devotion from him.

Panic welled up, and she tore away, stunned to realize tears stung her eyes. "I'm sorry," she rasped. "I can't do this."

But then she looked at him, at the blazing heat in his eyes, at the barely-controlled way he was breathing, and in an instant, they were tangled in each other's arms again.

Zhubaal backed her up, putting her spine against the wall and his erection against her belly. He kissed her hard as he rocked his hips into her, the ridge of his fly rubbing her through the fabric of her skirt. The friction was delicious, but it wasn't enough. It wouldn't be enough until they were naked.

She lifted one leg and hooked it around his thigh, moaning at the way his erection caressed her aching sex. His hand slid between them to cup her breast under her shirt, and she loved the way her skin tingled under his touch, little pops of ecstasy that made her gasp, especially when he pinched her nipple between his fingers.

"Oh...my," she moaned, arching against him.

"Is she in there?" he breathed against her ear.

"She?" Vex was so lust-punched that it took a heartbeat before she realized what he was asking. " Laura?" She rotated her hips, increasing the pressure between them, and that lovely, bone-melting wave of love washed over her again. "Yes. And she wants you. She wants you so badly."

He shuddered against her, trembling even harder when she dropped both hands to his incredibly firm ass and squeezed before sliding her fingers between his legs from behind to tease his balls.

"It's been so long," he murmured between desperate kisses against her throat. "So long since I've felt you against me."

"Too long," she agreed, not even knowing what she was saying or why she was saying it. But it felt right.

Which was wrong.

She frowned. There was actually something very wrong about all of this. The mincemeat tea must be working, because she couldn't feel the evil soul inside her...which meant she shouldn't be able to feel the lesser soul, either. But somehow, love and affection for this male filled her.

Had the evil soul lessened its grip on Laura's spirit?

"Zhubaal," she gasped. "We have to find Azagoth. Now."

His head snapped up, and if she hadn't felt the need for urgency, she'd have stripped him naked right then and there. His lips, kiss-swollen and glistening, beckoned to her, and she couldn't help but imagine them forging an erotic path down her body. And his eyes, God, his eyes, they were pools of the kind of lust a male reserved only for his lover. How she knew that, since she'd never been on the receiving end of that kind of intensity, she had no idea. All she knew was that in this single moment, he was her world.

And she was his.

Except she wasn't. *Laura* was his, and Vex was merely borrowing her emotions.

"Let's go," she pleaded. "Please. Hurry." *Before I decide to keep Laura's soul so I can experience this feeling every day.* "I think he can exorcise Laura now."

There was a split second of hesitation that made no sense, but then he took her hand and dragged her out of her room and down to the common area.

As they started across the courtyard toward Azagoth's palace, a *griminion* scurried past them, its little chittering noises muffled by its hood. Deep inside her, the evil spirit stirred, probably sensing the *griminion's* ability to collect souls. Shit. SuperEvil was going to grab Laura and hold her hostage again, and although a small part of Vex wanted to hold on to Laura as long as possible, it wasn't fair to Zhubaal or herself. What she was feeling for him right now wasn't real. It was on loan from Laura.

With a cry of frustration and sorrow, she jerked away from Zhubaal and summoned every ounce of willpower she had to expel the souls inside her, knowing the *griminion* would gather them up.

And miracle of miracles, she must have caught SuperEvil by surprise, because the other spirit broke loose and shot out of her body in a cloudy wisp. Instantly, the *griminion* wheeled around and captured the spirit with one bony hand. It shrieked as it struggled against the *griminion's* hold, but Vex knew from experience, from witnessing hundreds of *griminions* capture souls, that the spirit—presumably Laura—didn't have a shot of escaping.

Inside her, SuperEvil tore around, punching and biting and clawing, letting loose a psychic volley of anger and pain that nearly drove Vex to her knees. She swayed unsteadily, but Zhubaal caught her around the waist and braced her against his big body.

"There." She pointed at the *griminion* and the wildly flailing soul. "It's Laura. I don't know why she's not materializing as solid. You said in Sheoul-gra they have physical bodies."

"Yeah." He stared at the spirit, which had taken a vague humanoid shape. "But only in Azagoth's office and the Inner Sanctum." Still holding her against him, Zhubaal looked down at her. "You okay?"

Caught off guard by his concern, she nodded dumbly, and he released her, but only after making sure she wouldn't do a face plant. Cautiously, almost hesitantly, he moved to the spirit and reached out to it with a trembling hand.

Vex held her breath as his fingers passed through the cloud-like shadow. His shoulders fell, and she knew.

"It's not her," he choked out. "It's not Laura."

His devastation hit her like a seismic landslide. The concussive blast of anguish struck her in an almost physical blow, knocking her back a step.

But even as she recovered from his pain, a sick sensation bubbled up in her belly. "Laura must be the evil soul inside me."

"That's not possible." He sent the *griminion* away and turned to her. The devastation she'd felt from him showed in his face, and her chest hollowed out. "No matter what species of demon she was reborn as, she couldn't have been so corrupted. Not Laura."

Not Laura. He was so blind when it came to that stupid female, and Vex sighed. "I know you want to believe the best of her, but I'm telling you, the spirit inside me has to be her. I can still feel her affection for you." She lifted her gaze to his and fell right into those gorgeous eyes as if she'd always known them. "There's only one soul left inside me, Zhubaal. Evil or not, it's her."

"No," he ground out. "She would never—" He sucked in a sharp breath, and his eyes shot wide. "Oh...oh, damn."

"What?" The way he was looking at her freaked her the fuck out. "What is going on with you?"

"There's not one soul inside you," he said. "There are two."

She jammed one hand on her hip and held out her arm, which clearly bore only one soul-glyph. "I think I'd know if there was more than one—"

Abruptly he was in front of her, his hands gripping her shoulders, his gaze drilling into her with so much intensity she couldn't look away if she wanted to.

"There are two souls inside you, Vex. The evil one...and yours." With no warning, he kissed her. Captured her mouth in an erotic assault that brought tears to her eyes and joy to her heart. Her soul sang, like a violin that had finally found its bow. When he lifted his head and gazed into her eyes, she knew the truth before he even said it.

"It's you, Vex," he said hoarsely, and her breath left in a rush. "You're Laura."

Chapter Eight

Holy fucking shit.

Zhubaal couldn't believe it. After all this time and after all the false leads, he was looking at Laura. And he'd found her inside a flirty, brash, foul-mouthed *emim* who wasn't anything like the angel he'd pledged eternal faithfulness to. Not that he was going to complain. She could have been something far worse.

I've found her!

He dragged a ragged breath into his lungs and tried to let it all sink in. *Laura.* His heart thumped excitedly in his chest, but she didn't seem as thrilled. If anything, she seemed stunned, her body taut, her amethyst eyes glazed over.

"I know this must be a shock." The words fell out in a crazy rush. "And I know it sounds insane—"

"No, it doesn't." Shaking her head, she stepped away from him, and as much as he wanted to grab her, to hold onto her so she never left him again, he let her have her space. She hadn't had decades to prepare for this moment the way he had. But now that the moment was here, he realized that nothing could have prepared him for it. "I can feel it," she rasped. "God, I can feel *you.*" She swallowed. "It's freaking me out."

On impulse, he reached for her. "Laura—"

Wheeling out of his reach, she hissed. Actually *hissed* at him. "I'm Vex, not Laura." She jabbed an angry finger at him. "Let's get that straight right now. I don't know you, and you don't know me, and I don't care what kind of stupid damned oath Laura swore to you. *My lips did not speak the words.*"

Ice filled his chest cavity. He'd fantasized about this meeting, and while he'd considered the possibility that she wouldn't remember, in no imagined scenario had he thought she might reject who she was.

Fool. Did you think she'd give up her entire life to run into your arms? He broke out in a cold sweat as a horrifying possibility popped into his head.

"Do you have a mate?" he blurted. "A lover?" Because he'd have to kill the guy.

She folded her arms across her chest and glared. "Do you really think I'd offer to pull a stick out of your ass if I had a boyfriend?"

"Well, since I don't have a stick up my ass, I figured the offer wasn't genuine."

She shrugged. "I'll try anything once."

He had a feeling she was messing with him, and it left him off balance. He was used to Vex's unpredictable behavior and odd sense of humor, but now that he knew it was coming from Laura, it was throwing him.

Except she's not Laura.

But she was in there somewhere. Vex had admitted it when she said she had feelings for him.

"Look," he said, still reeling from all of this, "let's go to my place and talk. I have sweet mead. You used to like it."

"*I* don't know what the fuck you're talking about," she said crisply. "And Laura was a dolt. That shit is nasty."

Son of a bitch. His dreams of being reunited with Laura had not gone like this.

"Z!" Razr jogged toward them, and Zhubaal hated that he was relieved to have something other than this awkward situation to focus on. "I summoned that contractor you asked for. He said he can get the human cable channels you want. He said HBO comes in fuzzy, but—"

"Hey," he said, clapping Razr on the back to shut him up before Vex figured out that Z'd asked for more channels after she complained. "Thanks. Tell him it's all good. And will you take Laura—ah, Vex, to my quarters and stay with her? I need to talk to Azagoth."

Razr agreed, but Z didn't give Vex a chance to respond or argue. There was too much to say, and they both needed time for this to sink in. Especially Vex. He'd been searching for Laura for nearly a century, but obviously, she hadn't even known she was lost.

He should have expected that, should have expected how much it would hurt to find her and yet, somehow, to have lost her.

A knot of emotions tangled up inside him as he jogged to Azagoth's office. This should have been the best day of his life, but instead of being ecstatic, he was confused as hell, hurt, and angry.

It wasn't supposed to be like this. She was supposed to have remembered the oath, even if only on some subconscious level.

When he reached his boss's office, he threw open the door and strode into the center of the room. "You could have warned me."

"And you could have knocked." Azagoth sighed and looked up from the ledger he'd been writing in with a quill. "Warned you about what?"

"You know what," Z growled. "You could have told me that Vex is Laura."

Very slowly, Azagoth put down the pen and pegged him with a hard stare. "I told you Laura was inside Vex."

She's inside Vex. Okay, yeah, he'd said that. But it wasn't the same thing. "You said she was inside Vex. You didn't say she *was* Vex."

"Because she's *not* Vex. Vex is Vex. She *used* to be Laura."

"Dammit, Azagoth, you know what I mean." Z clenched his fists at his sides to keep from punching something that would get him turned into one of Azagoth's living statues. "You could have told me from the beginning so I didn't get blindsided, but you didn't, even though you knew."

"I *suspected*. I sensed that Vex's soul originated in Heaven. But it wasn't until I reached inside and touched it that I knew her soul was that of an Ipsylum, and there are very few of you."

"Why didn't you tell me, dammit? She was out for hours. Surely you could have found time to give me a, 'Hey, FYI, Vex and Laura are the same person.' I could have broken it to her without sounding insane and freaking her out."

Azagoth rose to his feet. "Does she have any memory of you?"

The question was like a blow to the heart. "No. Do you think it'll come back to her?" He tried not to hope, but he couldn't help but hold his breath as Azagoth walked around the desk and pulled a lever on the wall.

"I don't know," he said, as the wall panel slid back to reveal the cross-section of a tunnel. *Griminions* came from the right side of the tunnel, escorting souls through the portal on the left, but only after Azagoth had viewed each one. "Some people are gifted with soul-memory, some can access past-life memories through rituals or dreams, but others will never remember." He nodded approval as each soul passed, sending *griminions* through the tunnel in a steady stream.

Great. "So that's it? I'll always be a stranger to her?"

Azagoth looked at Z from over his shoulder and the soul parade halted. "Vex might never remember you, but her soul will." If Azagoth thought that was comforting, he was crazier than a ghastbat in the sunlight. "You're lucky she found her way here when she did. Jim Bob and Ricky Bobby saved her from one of Revenant's assassins."

Z's gut clenched. If the angels hadn't been there, he could have lost her. Again. And now he owed those two bastards. "She didn't say anything about that."

"She didn't know. They interrupted before the attack."

Damn. He'd forgotten that she would be in danger the moment she stepped outside of Sheoul-gra. "Can't you call Revenant or something?"

Azagoth snorted. "One does not simply *summon* the King of Hell." Z wondered if he'd be so la-de-da if it was Lilliana who was walking in the shadow of an executioner's ax.

"But you can contact him, right?"

Azagoth inclined his head. "I have ways."

"But you won't."

"I already have. He could be here by the time you get back from Los Angeles."

Of course. They still had to rid Vex of the evil soul that remained inside her. The thought that some vile demon had attached itself to her made him sick, and on the heels of that was anger and a desire to protect her at all costs.

"When do we leave?"

Azagoth produced a business card from out of his shirt pocket and flicked it into the air. Z caught it between two fingers.

"The address is on the card." Azagoth turned back to the soul tunnel, effectively dismissing him. "You leave now."

Chapter Nine

The journey to Beverly Hills via Harrowgates only took mere moments. Z would like to have flashed here, but his ability to travel in the blink of an eye was limited to places he already knew. Gates were almost as good though, invisible to humans and peppered all over the human and demon realms.

This particular gate opened up in a small, wooded park, and the moment Z and Vex stepped out, the bright sunshine nearly blinded him. How long had it been since he'd been anywhere but Sheoul?

Too long.

He generally avoided the human realm, not because he hated humans, but because they always reminded him of life before he lost his wings. He'd been free then. Well, as free as a warrior bound to his angelic Order and job could be, anyway. He'd gotten little time off, and he'd spent what free time he'd had with Laura. After he lost his wings and started working for Azagoth, he'd had just as little free time, and what he had was spent searching for Laura.

He glanced at her as they walked from the park toward the mansion where the demon they were going to see lived. She'd barely said two words to him since he'd picked her up from Razr and headed out. And didn't it just figure that now that Vex was finally behaving like Laura, he wanted Vex back. This sullen silence didn't suit her and only made the clack of her heels on the asphalt path more stark.

"Are you okay?" he asked as he guided her to a sidewalk that wound its way up a steep hill.

Vex sidestepped to avoid a low-hanging tree branch just off the path. "I don't know. This is a lot to take in." She glanced over at him. "You said Laura was Ipsylum. I'm still finding that hard to believe."

"She...*you*, didn't do well as a warrior. You didn't have the temperament for it."

She huffed. "Stop saying that. It wasn't me."

"Yes," he ground out, "it was. It was you before you were born as Vex. You were an angelic warrior, but not a very good one."

"All right," she said, her eyes flashing. "I'll play for now. I was Laura. So was the fact that I sucked as a warrior the reason I lost my wings?"

"Sort of," he said, ignoring her snippy tone. "You weren't built for violence. You were kind of like a lion who should have been a gazelle."

Vex frowned as they climbed a set of steps. "So how does a gentle gazelle get kicked out of Heaven?"

First, she'd been kicked out of the Ipsylum Order. But being an Ipsylum was more than just a job...it was truly a class of angel, and as much as Laura tried, she couldn't suppress instinct. And her instinct after being banished from not just her job but her family as well, was to rebel.

"She tried to fight the establishment," he said. "That rarely goes well." Not when the establishment consisted of a bunch of douchebag Archangels, Dominions, and Thrones who wanted to control everything. Z had to admit that as much as he'd loved Heaven, there was much more freedom in the human and demon realms.

Assuming one hadn't pledged loyalty to anyone. Like Azagoth.

It wasn't that Azagoth was a bad boss. Far from it. He was demanding but fair, cruel to enemies, but loyal to those he cared about. And the dude held a grudge. Hell, he'd only recently let Hades off the hook for something that had happened thousands of years ago. Azagoth's realm was his main priority, second only to Lilliana, and if your needs didn't square with that, too bad. If they did, he was happy to let you have whatever you wanted.

"So what happened to me?" She eyeballed him, a little more interested and less hostile now. "And how old was I?"

"We had just celebrated our fortieth name days when you were kicked out of the Ipsylum Order and joined a rebel group of angels who have been working to shift the balance of power in Heaven for thousands of years." He'd begged her to not get involved, but she'd been sure she could operate within the rebel faction without being caught.

"Now *that* sounds like me," she said with an impish grin that was pure Vex without a trace of Laura. "But why did she do it?"

"Archangels are in charge right now, but that hasn't always been the case," he said, watching a white delivery truck turn up the drive to the mansion. The sign on the side said, "Devilish Delights," and if the malevolent vibe coming off it was any indication, whatever was in that truck was bad news and not delightful at all. "Thrones used to rule the roost, with Dominions always struggling to gain more power and more control over everyone's lives, angel and human. But during the great Angel Rebellion, when Satan was ultimately cast out, Archangels took the opportunity to frame Thrones and Dominions as the bad guys, and they took over. Now there's a unified faction of angels of all Orders who want to overthrow the Archangels."

Vex rubbed her arm absently, and he wondered if the evil soul inside her was stirring. He'd given her another dose of suppressant before they left, but Azagoth had warned them that each dose was less effective than the one before it. "What does all of that have to do with Ipsylum?"

"I told you that Ipsylum are Heaven's special forces, but they're also Archangels' swords. When the other warrior angels are battling evil around the human realm, Ipsylum are battling evil within the angel ranks. So when an Ipsylum goes rogue, the Archangels act fast and with no mercy. You were caught plotting with the rebels before a year went by. Frankly, I'm surprised all you lost was your wings."

She frowned. "Were you...were we still together?"

He swallowed hard as the memories assaulted him. "Even as I held you in my arms after your wings were severed, you told me you loved me." Angels had dragged him away from her, but he'd fought so hard they'd had to chain him and bind his wings. It had taken years to find her again, but he'd been too late. She was dead, and he spent decades hunting the bastards who had killed her.

"It must have been hard for you."

It had been devastating. "Hard enough for me to lose my wings and family over it."

A warm breeze mussed her hair, creating spiky peaks he wanted to smooth with his palm. So very different from Laura's long blonde tresses, and he wasn't so sure it was a bad thing. "You really loved me...ah, her."

Okay, yeah, it was time to revert back to the *her, she,* and *you* part of the story. "She was my world," he said softly. Now he had to figure out how to fit Vex into that world.

But what if she didn't fit? The very thought put a knot in the pit of his gut.

"What was she like?"

He smiled. "She was beautiful," he said, but that didn't take away anything from Vex, who was stunning in a different way. Hell, he couldn't keep his eyes off the narrow strip of exposed flesh between the top of her boots and the hem of her skirt. Every time a breeze ruffled the pleats, he caught a glimpse of her fine, toned ass and silk underwear. "She had blonde hair and blue eyes, rare among Ipsylum. And she had the most amazing wings." All Ipsylum had the same deep burgundy wings, but hers had been tipped with silver, as if they'd been dipped in glitter. "We were born in the same year, so we grew up together."

They'd done everything together, from learning to fight to learning to fly. Thankfully she'd been better at flying than fighting, because more than once her agility and speed in the air had saved her life when her pathetic battle skills failed.

He stopped at the gated entrance to a massive mansion. To humans, this was the residence of Rowan Arch, a rich, influential Hollywood producer. But to demons, this was the lair of a powerful fallen angel who, while in the human realm, was capable of commanding human and demon spirits to do his bidding. But his true gift was his ability to drain power from souls to strengthen his own abilities. Azagoth hoped he could weaken the soul inside Vex enough for him to remove it.

"How do we get inside?"

"Rowan installed his own Harrowgate."

She whistled low and long. "He must be a serious badass with a shit-ton of money or human sacrifices or something. They don't give out private Harrowgates to just anyone."

No, they didn't. He looked around until he saw the telltale shimmer of a gate against the backdrop of the stone perimeter wall. "There."

The gate dropped them directly inside Rowan's manor. At least, he assumed he was inside the manor. They'd materialized in a huge, cold room more suited to a slaughterhouse than a rich dude's McMansion. Meat hooks hung from the ceiling, bloodstains darkened the concrete, and at least a dozen demons and humans waited for an audience with Rowan behind an iron fence on both sides of the room.

Azagoth had assured Zhubaal that he and Vex wouldn't have to wait, and he hoped his boss was right. He didn't want to be here any longer than he had to.

Ramreel demons armed with crossbows and swords stood watch near the double doors on the far side of the gymnasium-sized room, and two pasty-skinned, eyeless Silas demons roamed around, their creepy presence keeping the other waiting demons in line.

Vex leaned over and said quietly, "Whatever you do, don't kill anyone."

"Why not?"

Her gaze shot around the room, and he got the impression she was logging every weapon, cataloguing every individual, preparing for the worst. He could almost believe that she'd retained their Ipsylum training, except that Laura had never been this observant or prepared.

"Because the souls will jump inside me before Azagoth's *griminions* can get here."

Ah, good point.

"Also," she added, "if the bitchface inside me possesses my body...kill me."

He turned his head so fast his neck cracked. "What?"

Stopping in the middle of the room, she grabbed his arm and yanked him close. "I can't go through it again. If Azagoth can't exorcise the demon, kill me." She squeezed his biceps, digging her nails into his skin. "Don't make me beg. If you love Laura as much as you say you do, you won't want her to do the things this demon will force her to do. Please."

Please don't let them kill me.

He closed his eyes, once again hearing the words Laura had spoken to him while they'd waited for the Archangels' judgment the day she lost her wings. He hadn't let her die then, and he wouldn't now.

Opening his eyes, he pinned her with a hard stare. "Azagoth won't fail," he swore.

"If he does—"

"He won't."

She opened her mouth to argue more, he was sure, but snapped it shut as a Ramreel approached them, his armor clanking as loudly as his hoofed feet.

"Mr. Arch will see you now." He focused his small eyes on Vex, and Z bristled. "Female. I would extract payment...from you."

"Payment?" Vex produced a blade from who-knew-where and held it casually at her hip. Damn, she was fast. Laura would have cut herself. And she wouldn't be standing there, shifting her weight into an attack stance and readying for a fight. Z held back, prepared to obliterate this asshole now that he had his powers in the human realm but wanting to see how Vex handled it first. "What kind of payment? And for what?"

"For allowing you through the Harrowgate," he said, his gray lips turning up in a grotesque sneer. "There was a sign at the entrance."

"Yeah, well, we missed the sign," Z said, "so back the fuck off."

"I will have payment." The Ramreel, a good two feet taller than Zhubaal, swung his massive head back around to Vex and stomped his hoof on the floor. "You will only scream for a minute."

Z had always prided himself on his self-control, but both pride and self-control got tossed out the window when Laura was threatened. Vex had warned him not to kill anyone, but he welcomed the rush of power that funneled to his fingertips, ready to burst from him in a searing stream of hellfire.

His leathery wings flared high as he stepped between the Ramreel and Vex, his fingers flexing with the desire to destroy.

"Touch her," he said, his voice scraping gravel, "and I will rend you limb from limb and then fuck your dying corpse as you bleed out."

The Ramreel's hand tightened on the giant mace he carried, and Z wondered if the sheep-brained idiot was stupid enough to take a swing.

Just as Z prepared to take a pre-emptive strike, the demon shrugged and lumbered off.

"Wow," Vex breathed.

Zhubaal nodded. "Yeah, powerful stuff, huh?"

"Well, it's quite the visual." She flipped the blade between her fingers before sliding it into her boot. "I mean, I'm assuming you won't take the time to strip him before you draw and quarter him, which means that to fuck his dying body, you'll have to take off his bloody pants. That'll be really awkward, you know?" He stared at her, almost unable to believe this was truly Laura. "What? I'm just saying that to make a threat effective, you've got to think it through."

"It was off the cuff," he said, exasperated.

"Clearly."

He ground his teeth. Vex's new name suited her. Just as he was about to tell her that, the double doors at the other end of the room opened, and a human in a tuxedo beckoned them inside.

"You ready?"

There was a fierceness in her gaze that he couldn't help but admire, so he was taken aback when she shook her head. "I don't know."

"What do you mean you don't know?" he asked, incredulous. "This might be your only chance to get rid of the demon you're carrying around inside you."

"And it'll also make me beholden to Azagoth for the rest of my life."

"But you'll be alive," he pointed out. "He'll protect you from Revenant's forces."

The look she gave him, one of sadness and maybe a touch of revulsion, made his heart sink. "But what is life if you're bound to someone all the way to your soul?" she asked quietly.

He stiffened. "You mean like we are to each other?"

"Exactly." She rubbed her arms as if cold, but it was about a thousand degrees in the room. "I can feel you, Zhubaal. I feel so much love for you, but it's not mine. It's hers. It's Laura's. So you can understand why I can't enter into a contract like Azagoth's so lightly." She met his gaze with a steely one of her own. "Not when I wish I could break the one with you."

Chapter Ten

The devastation in Zhubaal's expression tore Vex apart. He didn't deserve what she'd said, but it was the truth. She was still reeling from everything that had happened in the last couple of days, and she suspected she'd still be reeling tomorrow. And the next day. And the next week, month, year...

I was an angel who pledged my eternal, everlasting love to the male standing beside me.

No, *Laura* had done that. Vex wasn't that stupid.

"Are you coming, or not?" The elderly tuxedo guy managed to look bored and annoyed at the same time as he stood in the doorway.

Zhubaal's expression was cold when he turned to her, and her stomach lurched. She'd hurt him deeply enough for him to shut down, and she wondered if Laura had ever done the same thing. Somehow, she doubted it.

"Well?" he asked, his voice as chilly as his gaze. "Would you rather work for Azagoth or take your chances with the demon inside you and Revenant's forces?"

Obviously, she had to choose Azagoth. She just didn't like it, and she wanted to at least feel as if she had some control in the matter.

She started toward Tux, relieved when she heard Zhubaal's heavy footsteps behind her.

The chamber they entered was nothing like Vex would have expected. This guy was some sort of super wizard or something, so she figured his lair would look like a movie cliché...the way most sorcerers' lairs really looked.

But Rowan had money and taste, and the room they entered could have been a museum of demonic art and artifacts. Haunting paintings by noted demon and even angelic artists lined the walls, and the shelves were practically sagging under the weight of stone statuettes, clay masks from various demon tribes, and carvings made from bones. Even the floor rugs had been woven in various styles and from various materials depending on the maker's species and culture.

If the chamber wasn't what Vex expected, Rowan was exactly what she'd expect from a fallen angel. Tall, dark, and handsome. Sure, his hair was platinum blond and his eyes were pale blue, but damn, the darkness emanating from him was intoxicating. It definitely made SuperEvil stir, sending a warm buzz to the tip of every nerve ending.

When she looked over at Z, she could tell he felt Rowan's power as well. His eyes gleamed with bloodlust and his hand had fallen to the sword at his side, as if he was ready to do battle.

She shivered in forbidden delight. A battle between two fallen angels would be something to see.

"You're turned on." Zhubaal's voice, low and so close to her ear she nearly jumped, went through her like a purr.

"Does that disgust you?"

"No." For some reason, he sounded mad, like he wanted to be disgusted but wasn't.

"Hello." Rowan, dressed in a black sweater and khakis, moved toward them so smoothly he glided. "I have been waiting for you."

"For what, ten minutes?" Z asked.

Rowan blinked before giving Zhubaal a wary once-over. "Yes." He smiled, flashing fangs. "Azagoth sent word that you are in need of this." He held up a vial of black liquid.

"And that is?" she asked.

"It will force the soul inside you to the surface, where Azagoth will be able to exorcise it without killing you."

Zhubaal paced around the room, hand still on the hilt of his sword as he studied the decor. "Why is this potion necessary?"

Rowan's smile made SuperEvil vibrate with desire, and Vex clenched her teeth, concentrating on keeping the demon down.

"Because Vex has the soul of an angel but the body of a lesser being. That allows some of the oldest, most evil demons to access an incredibly powerful soul and cement themselves to those who are mistakenly called, "living.""

"Mistakenly?" She snorted. "I'm quite alive, thank you."

He laughed. "Ours are borrowed bodies, subject to decay and death. Souls are our true forms, solid in Heaven and in Sheoul-gra. But the Dark Lord will one day rule the demon and human realms, where all souls will be solid, eternal, and subject to great suffering."

SuperEvil felt such pleasure at his words that Vex nearly gasped at the flood of orgasmic sensation at her core. Somehow she managed to offer a sarcastic smile. "Gee, yes, that sounds great. Now, how does the potion work?"

"You will drink it, but only in Azagoth's presence." He handed it to her, and she was surprised that it was hot enough to be uncomfortable in her hand. "The demon inside you will react according to the species it identifies with, and you will have no way to control it. Azagoth will be your only hope of stopping it."

Zhubaal cursed under his breath. "The demon is a succubus."

Rowan laughed. "Then Azagoth can have some fun while he's...taking her."

A growl erupted, a sound Vex could only describe as something being dragged against its will from the pits of hell, and suddenly Zhubaal was in the other fallen angel's face, the tip of his sword jammed into Rowan's throat.

"You will not speak that way about her." Black veins rose to the surface of Zhubaal's skin as his anger brought out the *fallen* part of the angel in him.

SuperEvil began to vibrate violently under her skin as her excitement level rose. A hum blasted Vex's eardrums, growing so loud she could no longer hear either Zhubaal or Rowan, who seemed to be in a fang-ridden snarl-fest.

It was so hot.

No! It wasn't hot. It was dangerous and violent and...oh, God, heat flushed her body and flowed in electric currents to her breasts and pelvis. Desire overwhelmed her, and she ripped off her top before she knew what was happening.

Stop! But she couldn't. The soul was taking over, wrestling control away from her while using the furious energy created by the two fallen angels to do it.

"Stop," she gasped, but the males didn't seem to hear. Zhubaal had Rowan up against the wall now, and there was blood on the floor and on Rowan's face and all she wanted to do was tear off the rest of her clothes and put her naked body between them.

We'll fuck them both. SuperEvil's voice clanged in her ears. *We'll hurt them, make them like it, and when it's done, one will kill the other.*

Vex tried to scream, tried to warn Zhubaal. But she was drowning in a pool of oily malevolence, unable to surface, and all she could do was scream inside her head as SuperEvil held her under and set its sights on Zhubaal.

Chapter Eleven

The smell of blood and danger hung heavy in the air, electrifying it, giving Zhubaal a power punch of adrenaline that jacked him into battle mode. Rowan hissed through bloody fangs, a happy result of Zhubaal's right hook.

Oh, this had only been a scuffle so far, two alpha males testing each other, but Zhubaal knew where he stood. Rowan was strong, a fallen angel with the kind of power that would make even very evil demons piss themselves.

But Z was stronger, and Rowan knew it.

"You care far too much for the female," Rowan gritted out. "It will be your downfall."

That was probably true, but it didn't mean Z wanted to hear it. Especially not from some sleazeball who promised fools fame and fortune if they gave up their firstborns or their mothers or whatever it was Rowan asked for in return.

"And you care too much about running your mouth," Zhubaal said. "That will be *your* downfall." He pressed upward with his blade, puncturing the delicate skin just under the bastard's chin. The fresh stream of blood made his cock hard and his balls throb...no, wait.

He frowned, confused by the powerful sexual need coursing through him. Rowan seemed as perplexed, and they both gasped when a sexual wave crashed into them in an almost physical blow that knocked the air from his lungs. What the—

Fuck.

He wheeled around, and his mouth dropped open. Vex was sauntering toward them, naked except for her thigh-high boots, her hands cupping her full breasts as her thumbs flicked across the nipples. Holy shit, it was the most erotic yet inappropriately timed thing he'd ever seen.

"Your blood," she purred. "I want to bathe in it while I fuck you."

His entire body jerked in shock. *Oh...shit.* The succubus had possessed Vex. He'd failed to protect her, and now she was paying for it.

Panic made his breath burn in his throat. "Vex, listen to me."

"She can't hear you." Succubus Vex cocked her head. "But how sweet...I can feel her love for you. She'll be pissed when she finds out your cock was inside me and that *I* gave you the best fuck of your life." She slid her hand between her legs, and next to him Rowan made a sound of lusty approval.

Very calmly, and without even looking, Z shoved his sword through the male's belly. It wouldn't kill him, but it should take the edge off his libido. And if that didn't do it, castration would.

Rowan shouted in agony and stumbled backward, his feet slipping in his own blood. The doors burst open and his army of Ramreels and Silas demons poured inside, weapons ready.

Time to go. He darted toward Vex, but she spun away, grabbing a dagger from her pile of clothes in a fluid sweep.

"Vex!"

In a graceful surge, she danced between several of the demons, slashing and stabbing, somehow avoiding their blows. Three fell, holding their guts as they spilled out of their bellies.

Son of a bitch, she was good. She'd eviscerated two of those guys with the heels of her boots.

A Silas swung at Vex with a studded club while her back was turned. Z flashed in, catching the bastard by the wrist before the blow landed. With a quick twist, he snapped the demon's arm and flung him into a gang of guards running toward them.

"Gotta go, Vex!" They had to escape this clusterfuck before one of the dying demons croaked and got sucked into her. He snatched the potion from off the floor where she'd dropped it before seizing her around the waist as he flashed them out of there.

At least, flashing out of there was the plan. It didn't happen. Instead, momentum launched them into the wall.

"Shit!" He cursed as his shoulder wrenched hard in the collision. "The place is warded!" He should have known. Rowan would have to be an idiot to not ward his lair from unauthorized entrance and exit.

Vex wrenched around and punched him in the jaw. His head snapped back, but he held onto her as he bulldozed through the guards, sending them scattering with a blast of searing energy that shot out of him in a three-hundred-and-sixty-degree shockwave.

"Release me!" the Vex-thing screamed, clawing and biting as he half-dragged, half-carried her to the exit.

He ignored her, blasting two more demons with enough juice to blow them apart and throw bone shrapnel into the poor bastards who had been waiting to see Rowan. Vex hurled herself away from him, but in a stroke of luck, she slammed into the door, shoving it open and giving him a chance to catch her before the spirits of the demons he'd just killed got drawn into her.

Swinging her into his arms, he flashed out of there, but as he did, he caught a glimpse of Rowan out of the corner of his eye and felt the bite of a lightning strike against his hip. His yelp of pain disappeared behind them as they materialized on the landing pad inside Sheoul-gra, his status as a resident allowing him to bypass the ward that kept everyone else from flashing in or out.

Razr was there almost instantly, sprinting across the courtyard. He shouted at a nearby Memitim, who darted toward Azagoth's palace.

"Don't touch her." Still struggling to hold onto her, Zhubaal snapped his wings around her, shielding her from all eyes but his.

Azagoth flashed in, his eyes swallowed entirely by inky blackness. "The potion," he rumbled. "She needs to drink it."

Z couldn't do much with his arms wrapped around Vex, so he flipped the vial into the air with his fingers. Azagoth caught it, popped the stopper, and forced the contents into her mouth. He snapped her jaw shut and stepped back, somehow keeping her from opening her mouth to spit out the potion even from a distance.

"Swallow," he growled, and Vex snarled and thrashed, but obeyed. Azagoth's black marble eyes rolled up to meet Z's gaze. "Hold her steady and put away your wings."

Neither was easy to do, but he stashed his wings and held her tight, her body pressed against his. Still, she was freakishly strong and squirmy, and there was no way he could do this by himself.

But there was also no way he was allowing Razr—or anyone—to touch her. She rocked her head back, smashing her skull into his nose. Pain shattered his face, and she did it again, layering the agony with another skillful blow. And another.

Son of a...*fuck*! A stab of red-hot fire went through his foot and up his leg. *She stabbed me in the foot with the heel of her fucking boot.* The thought barely had time to form before her other boot came at him. He kicked his leg back and she stomped the ground hard, missing his boot by a hair.

"Azagoth," he hissed. "Hurry!"

"Hold her still," Azagoth roared.

On impulse, he bared his fangs and bit into her throat. He'd used his fallen angel fangs in battle before, and he supposed this counted as a fight. But this was different. Always before, the taste of his enemy's blood enraged him, fueling the violence and his strength. But Vex's blood energized him. Aroused him. He knew that, for many fallen angels, feeding wasn't a necessity, but its application for pleasure was well known. By everyone but Zhubaal.

Until now.

As Vex's silky blood flowed over his tongue, he felt her relax. It was subtle, a mere drop of one shoulder and the tiniest shift of her head to allow him more access, but it was enough to give Azagoth the break he needed.

His fist punched through her chest. She screamed, and if Z's mouth hadn't been locked on her throat, he'd have screamed, too. Now he knew why Azagoth had wanted him to wait in the hall last time. Seeing her agony, *feeling* her agony, tore him to shreds. Laura had been killed this way. Vex had suffered through it in Azagoth's office and now, again, while Z was letting it happen.

Seething hatred for the one hurting her rose up, and although it made no sense, he wanted to kill Azagoth for this. His wings shot out from his back as if they had minds of their own and his fangs pulsed as desire to kill the thing causing Vex's pain consumed him.

Azagoth roared, and all around them the air went still. The trees closest to them exploded as if they'd been struck by lightning, and the water in the courtyard fountain blasted upward.

Rearing back, Azagoth ripped a cloudy, shapeless mass from Vex's chest. As if the realm was breathing a sigh of relief, everything returned to normal, and Azagoth flashed away with the succubus's spirit.

Vex collapsed against him, and he scooped her into his arms. Very gently, he wrapped his wings around her, shielding her from the view of the Memitim and Unfallen who had gathered to watch the show.

He glanced over at Razr. "I'm taking her to my quarters. See that someone brings some food. Maybe some broth."

Razr bowed and took off as Z headed toward the mansion. He could have flashed to his quarters, but he didn't want to give up even a second of holding Vex like this.

Moaning, she wrapped one arm around his shoulder to help support herself.

"Is it over?" she whispered. "Did I shame myself?"

A chill sliced through Z. She'd asked the same question after her wings had been severed. She'd laid in his arms, bleeding and quaking, worried that, in her haze of pain and fear, she'd sobbed or pleaded for a deal or begged for mercy.

"No," he said hoarsely, just as he had all those years ago. But this time he didn't have to lie. "You didn't."

She smiled weakly up at him. "I'm naked."

Laughing, he pulled his wings tighter around her as they mounted the steps. "I noticed."

"Did you like it?" She rested her head against his neck, and the intimacy of it made his heart lurch.

"Except for the gaping hole in your chest."

"What?" She struggled to look down at herself but he caught her chin with his thumb and lifted her face to his.

"I'm kidding." Tenderly, because she was probably sore all over, he pressed a lingering kiss into her hair. He loved how her spiky locks tickled his lips. "Well, you did have a gaping hole, but it's healed."

"Good." She yawned. "Make love to me."

He missed a step, stumbled, and flashed them to his quarters before they did a face plant. Standing in the middle of his palatial living room, he stared down at her. "What?"

"We've waited a long time, don't you think?"

Holy shit, was she serious? His dick believed her, and if he didn't put her down in the next couple of seconds, she'd know it. "A hundred and forty years." And two months, three weeks, and six days, counting from the year they were born, of course.

She gave him an impish grin. "I was thinking a couple of days."

Folding away his wings, he laughed again. Before Vex came into his life, how long had it been since he'd laughed?

Over a hundred years, probably.

"Come on," he said, holding her tighter as he strode down the hall to one of the five bedrooms. Azagoth wouldn't earn any accolades for providing lavish living wages, but he was generous with the perks. "You need to rest and finish healing."

She tried to hide another yawn behind her hand. "Do not."

"Do." He took her straight to the shower, where, fully clothed, he held her under the hot, cleansing spray. She didn't seem to mind, merely settled her head against his chest as the blood and the day's events flowed down the drain.

After drying her, he took her to his bed, leaving a trail of water from his soaked clothes behind. The king-sized four-poster took up only a small part of the master bedroom, most of which was a waste of space. The reading nook was cozy, he supposed, but he rarely had the time to use it. Until now, all of his free time had been spent looking for Laura. The hot tub, built seamlessly into the polished white marble floor and fed by hot springs from Sheoul, filled another nook, but again, it went mostly unused.

"Nice place." She winced as she burrowed under the covers, reaffirming his conviction that she needed to finish healing. "Do you know what kinds of things we could do in that hot tub?" As he drew the comforter up to cover her shoulders, she winked. "I can snorkel."

His cock twitched as his wet pants got really fucking tight. "Maybe later," he croaked. "I'm going to change clothes and get you some ice water—"

Her fingers closed around his wrist. "Stay," she said softly. "Please. Lay down with me."

There was no reason for his reluctance, but he hesitated anyway.

Only a couple of hours ago she'd wished she had never exchanged vows of loyalty with him, and now she wanted him to stay with her when she was exhausted, in pain, and vulnerable.

We're both vulnerable. And really fucked up.

Vex loved him with Laura's love. He loved Laura, but how much of Vex was Laura?

He wondered if Underworld General Hospital had mental health specialists on staff, because they both might need an appointment.

Vex squeezed his wrist, prompting an answer. "Yeah. I'll stay." He looked down at his dripping clothes. "I have to change first."

"Just take off your clothes. We can be naked together."

His heart gave an excited thump, which was followed by an immediate breakout of a cold sweat. What if he couldn't control himself? Oh, he wasn't going to attack her, but he wasn't sure he could resist her, either. She might have been kidding about them waiting for a long time, but he hadn't been joking at all.

"Oh, criminy," she mumbled. Her heavy lids closed, and her voice began to fade as she spoke. "Have you always been this uptight?"

"No," he said as he shed his clothes, doing his best to keep turned so she couldn't see his trembling fingers. Or his erection. "I used to be worse."

That wasn't a joke, either.

His heart was pounding as he climbed under the covers with her. He'd never been naked with a female before, and his body was telling him all about it. His skin was so hypersensitive he could feel every individual thread in the eighteen-hundred-thread count sheets. His lungs were pushing air in and out like he needed oxygen to run a marathon. And his cock was as hard as the marble hot tub he never used.

Although Vex didn't open her eyes again and her breathing settled instantly into a deep, easy pattern, she slid her hand across the mattress to find his. His heart sang.

His Laura was home.

Chapter Twelve

Vex would really like it if the next time she woke up she wasn't in a strange place, in a strange bed. At least this time she woke up alone in her body. There were no parasitic souls inside her. Just...peace.

Smiling, she rolled over.

And bumped into a warm body.

Startled, she opened her lids and found herself looking into the most gorgeous eyes she'd ever seen. "Zhubaal," she whispered.

He shifted, propping himself up on one elbow. "Hey." He reached out and brushed a knuckle over her cheek with so much tenderness she nearly wept. "How are you feeling?"

"My chest hurts a little, but otherwise, good." Her smile faltered. "But I don't remember anything after—" She broke off, horrified as the memories filtered back into her brain. "Oh, God, the succubus possessed me."

"It's okay. It wasn't for long."

"Did I...did I hurt anyone?"

"Only scumbags." He snorted. "And damn, woman, I'd want you on my battlefield any day."

His compliment gave her warm fuzzies. "Bet you never said that to Laura."

"No," he said, and the troubled expression on his face made her regret her words. He still loved Laura, and Vex definitely was not her. Well, technically she was, but not in any way it mattered.

"So," she said as she tentatively trailed her finger over the back of his hand. "Where do we go from here?"

"You," he said, "are going to soak in the hot tub. It'll be good for your aching muscles. I'm going to get us breakfast."

She glanced over at the tub that could easily hold Zhubaal and ten girlfriends, and a twinge of jealousy tweaked her. Actually, no, it was a giant wave of jealousy, and it crashed over her like a tsunami.

Before she could stop herself, she blurted, "How many females have you had in that thing?"

He jerked, taken aback. "None."

Oh, right. That crazy vow of loyalty. Still, she blinked, amazed that he hadn't taken advantage of all the delights to be had in a steaming pool with bubbling jets. "You have some seriously amazing willpower," she mused. "Because I'd make daily use of that sucker."

A shadow passed over his expression, and damn it, she just realized what she'd said. He'd been faithful to Laura all this time, and in this weird, twisted reality he lived in, she was Laura, and she *hadn't* been faithful.

Way to jam a dagger straight into his heart.

"Hey," she said, reaching for him. "I didn't mean it."

He shrugged off her touch, and in the shadowy light from a lamp in the reading nook, she saw his expression turn savage. "How many males have you been with?"

No, this wasn't uncomfortable at all. "Zhubaal, I don't think—"

"How. Many."

Annoyed at his tone and the question, she sat up, not caring that the sheet fell away to expose her breasts. "That," she said firmly, "is none of your business. My life before I met you was my own. It's still my own. It was your choice to be celibate for all this time, and it was my choice to enjoy myself. I like sex, and I'm not ashamed of it. If you can't deal with that, it's your problem, not mine. Now," she said, whipping the sheet away to reveal her entire naked body, "do you want to make up for lost time?"

As expected, she'd just taken the edge off his anger. His eyes shot wide, going even wider as she spread her legs, just a little, to reveal a hint of her arousal. She was wet already, had been since she got to Sheoul-gra, and now she knew why. Oh, yes, she loved sex, but she'd never been drawn to any male as quickly and as feverishly as she had been to Zhubaal. Her healthy sex drive combined with the already established familiarity thanks to her past-life history, had made her want to have him inside her almost from the second she saw him.

She couldn't stand it anymore. Spreading her legs wide, she beckoned to him with one hand while sliding the other down her stomach. She watched him as her fingers found her cleft, loving how his nostrils flared and the veins in his neck stood out with every hard swallow.

"I'm waiting," she said in a teasing, singsong tone as she rubbed her hand back and forth over her smooth mound.

The blatant hunger in his expression fed her own, and she reached for him, intent on pulling him down on top of her, but to her shock, he reared back and scrambled off the bed. He stood next to it, his eyes wild, his chest heaving. Alarm rang through her, and she sat up.

"Zhubaal, what's wrong?"

Jamming his hand frantically through his hair, he shook his head. "This isn't how it was supposed to be."

"How what's not supposed to be?" Before the question was even out of her mouth, she knew. "This is about Laura."

He nodded. "I know you don't want to hear that—"

"It's okay," she said softly, surprising herself. Laura had proven to be a big pain in the ass, but she had been a huge part of Zhubaal's life, and Vex needed to accept it.

And he had to accept that she wasn't Laura.

No, she didn't know where this relationship was headed, but she did know she wanted to explore it. How could she not? She'd never felt as though anything was missing in her life, but the emotions he'd awakened in her couldn't be contained. They had a connection she couldn't deny, a connection that had been missing with every sexual partner she'd ever had.

Maybe that was why she'd never gotten serious with anyone. There'd never been even the most minimal connection. Maybe the stupid vow *had* affected her in this life. Because no matter how great the guy was, she'd never been able to make a relationship last for more than a couple of weeks. Even then, she'd only hung in for the sex. Emotions had never come into play.

"It's not okay." He scrubbed his hand over his face. "We were cheated out of everything we wanted. Our first time wasn't supposed to be like this."

She rolled her eyes. "Let me guess. You and Laura probably planned to make love for the first time on marshmallow clouds cradled by rainbows while listening to harp music." His defiant glare said she was pretty close to being on target. "We don't have clouds or rainbows here, but we have a big bed, all the right parts, and I take an herb that prevents pregnancy, so why don't you tell me what's really going on?" His nervous swallow made something in her brain click, and without thinking, she blurted, "Zhubaal...are you...a virgin?"

Cheeks bright with embarrassment, he averted his gaze and nodded. "She wanted to wait until we were wed."

This isn't how it was supposed to be.

Of course it wasn't. He'd expected his first time to be with someone inexperienced. Probably shy. And here Vex was, ready to get raunchy and do things that would probably have given Saint Laura the vapors.

Well, there was plenty of time to be naughty. Right now, Zhubaal needed a gentler touch. And she wanted his first time to be special. She couldn't be Laura, but she could at least give him that.

She'd be *honored* to give him that.

Slowly, so he wouldn't feel trapped, she wrapped herself in the blanket at the foot of the bed and scooted over so she was on her knees on the mattress in front of him. They were equal height like this, allowing her to look him directly in the eyes.

"Now," she said softly, "tell me how it was supposed to be." Holding the blanket closed with one hand, she cupped his cheek with the other. He stiffened, but at least he didn't pull away. She leaned in, until she was a mere inch from his lips. "I assume you planned to start by kissing?"

He hesitated, and her gut dropped. She wanted this more than she'd ever wanted anything. Her first time had been a drunken fumble-fest with Brad Fisher, captain of the high school football team, in the backseat of his car, and she'd never really taken it slow with anyone.

She wasn't one for cuddling or being romantic, and she'd always been more about the goal than the journey to get there.

But for the first time, the journey *was* the goal.

"Yes," he finally said, closing the distance between their mouths. His kiss was unsure at first, so delicate that his lips could have been butterfly wings. But as she melted into him, he deepened the kiss, his tongue sweeping along the seam of her lips. Like a total pro, he slid his hand around to her neck, caressing her skin, kneading her into putty.

"And then?" she murmured against his mouth.

He nipped her bottom lip, the pinch of pain shooting straight to her core and making her moan. "And then I'd strip her."

Pulling back, he peeled her fingers from the blanket. It fell away, pooling around her knees. His gaze raked her, and she held her breath. What did he think of her? Did her body match up to Laura's? Shit. She wasn't used to being self-conscious, but then, she wasn't used to being reincarnated, either.

"You're so beautiful," he said, his voice as thick with need as his cock, which jutted upward in a graceful arc that made her mouth water.

"Now what?" *Please say you want me to take you in my mouth.*

"Kiss me again." Somehow, that was even better, and her heart fluttered with happiness. He stepped into her until his knees hit the mattress and his erection pressed into her belly, her breasts into his chest. "Like you mean it."

She slanted her mouth over his. "I mean it," she whispered, wrapping her arms around his shoulders.

He kissed back, hard, his tongue pushing past her lips and teeth to thrust against hers. One arm came around her back to brace her as he lifted her up and laid them both down on the bed so he was half-on, half-off of her, one big leg tucked between hers. All the while, he kissed her senseless, never breaking contact. But as he gripped her hip to tug them closer together, he raised his head and looked down at her, his gaze glowing with need.

"I want to explore you," he said, and she grinned, desire spiraling wildly through her. Now he was talking.

Still, she didn't want to come across as too forward...not yet, anyway. She'd definitely introduce him to her adventurous, uninhibited side, but later.

She slid her hand over the firm muscles in his back to the even firmer muscles in his ass and gave him a playful squeeze. "Explore all you want."

Beneath his skin, he quivered. God, she loved his reactions to her. Loved how he closed his eyes and inhaled deeply, as if grounding himself in this moment before dropping his mouth to her throat. He nuzzled her, kissing and licking, as he cupped her breast in one hand.

She arched into his touch, telling him without words that he didn't need to treat her like a fragile piece of crystal. He got the hint, caressing her breast with more pressure, flicking and pinching her nipple with his fingers as he kissed a hot path from her neck to collar bone. His hips rolled slowly, rubbing his erection against her hip, mimicking what she wanted him to do between her legs.

Her sex throbbed at the thought, and she bit back a growl of frustration. Then he sucked her breast into his mouth, and she sighed with pleasure. Gently, he swirled his tongue around her swollen nipple as he shifted to cup both breasts, massaging and stroking.

"That's so good," she moaned, and he smiled against her skin.

He worked his way lower, kissing as he went. But as his lips found the hollow of her belly, he slowed, as if he wasn't sure how she'd react if he kept going. To help him along, she shifted and spread her legs so he was forced to settle between them.

Taking her cue, he dragged his tongue down until he reached the top of her cleft. His hands trembled as he wrapped them around her thighs and pulled her open for his hungry gaze. The tips of his fangs peeked out from his parted lips, and she suddenly wanted him to bite her. She'd slept with a guy with fangs once, but she hadn't allowed him to penetrate her with them.

Zhubaal could use his any way he wanted to.

He licked his lips, his eyes feasting on her waiting flesh. "I'm not sure..."

"Yes," she said quickly. "You're sure. You can do it. *Please* do it." God, his tongue was *made* to do it.

His smoldering gaze snapped up to hers. "Oh, I plan to." He flicked his tongue over a fang, and her breath left her in a rush. "I'm just not sure she would have let me."

Laura was a fucking fool. "I'll let you do anything you want," she murmured, and then she lost her voice as he lowered his mouth to her core and his warm breath bathed her in shivery sensation.

His tongue slipped out to taste her so delicately she barely felt it. It was so sweet the way he was exploring so gently, but she wasn't made of eggshells. Still, this was his first time, and he needed to find his way.

He kissed her lightly, maddeningly lightly. His lips feathered over her, nibbling but not tasting. He scooted down so he could adjust his hands to lift her hips, spreading her wider as her legs fell open. When his lips touched her again, it was with another delicate kiss before he tilted his head and drew his tongue up the crease between her sex and her thigh.

So close, and yet...she whimpered at his diabolical torture.

He explored her relentlessly, licking and kissing her inner thighs and the outer-most regions of her sex, teased her so well that when his tongue finally clipped her clit, she cried out and startled him.

"Are you okay?"

"No," she breathed, shoving his head back down. "You stopped. Not okay."

He chuckled against her, his lips tickling her before he opened his mouth over her core and licked her with the flat of his tongue. She cried out again as the tip flicked over her hypersensitive knot of nerves.

"You taste like ambrosia," he whispered against her core. "I *love* this."

Not nearly as much as she did.

Bolder now, he lapped at her with increasing enthusiasm, varying his speed and the pattern of his tongue, and she came off the bed when he plunged it deep inside and swirled it while she squirmed and thrashed.

"Tell me what you want." His voice was a guttural, resonant growl that shivered through all her feminine parts.

"Just keep doing what you're doing." She spoke between halting, panting breaths. "But stroke yourself while you're doing it. I want to see how you jerk off," she breathed, "so I can do it for you later."

His head popped up, his half-lidded eyes blinking. For a heartbeat she thought she'd crossed some sort of *Laura wouldn't do this* line that would snap him out of what they were doing. But an eager rumble rose up in his throat as he palmed his cock and dropped his head between her legs again.

Oh...*yes.* She couldn't really see him stroking himself, but she loved imagining his hand wrapped around that thick erection, the fat, plum head pumping in and out of his fist. His tongue lashed at her, dipping inside her and circling her clit, but when he latched on and sucked, she couldn't take it anymore.

She shouted in ecstasy, the climax ripping her apart over and over. He might not be experienced, but he had one hell of an erotic instinct.

Which he proved by licking her gently, bringing her down slowly until she was too sensitive to handle it. He pressed his lips against her in a final, lingering kiss, and when he lifted his head, the hunger in his eyes nearly undid her again.

A soft growl rattled the air as he prowled his way up her body, his gaze locked on hers, the tips of his fangs visible between his glistening lips.

"That was amazing," she said hoarsely.

"I don't know what I'm doing." He paused to lap at her breast. "But I like learning. I like listening to how your breathing changes depending on what I'm doing with my tongue. I could do that for hours."

Oh, jackpot.

"I'd let you do that for hours." She reached between them and found his cock. As her fingers closed around it, he moaned. Smiling, she guided him to her entrance. But just as the blunt tip touched her heated flesh, he locked up, his body trembling.

"Zhubaal?" She stroked his neck, and he let out a little purr that rumbled all her erogenous zones. "What is it?"

He looked down at her. "I'm savoring this." He pushed his hips forward, just enough for the head of his cock to dip inside her, and he moaned. "Also, I don't want to embarrass myself." His sex-swollen lips tipped up in a self-deprecating smile, and then his head fell back as he lowered himself between her legs.

When he was fully inside her, their bodies connected, a strange, incredible energy seemed to form a circuit between them. Her brain shorted out, flashing not images, but emotions that they had once shared. Together. And that was when she knew. Knew that this was a moment over a hundred years in the making. Whatever minor doubts she'd had were gone. Vex had never believed in soul mates, but as her soul touched Zhubaal's, she knew the truth.

They belonged together.

Chapter Thirteen

Perfection. There wasn't another word that could so adequately describe the feeling of being joined with Vex this way. Watching him with half-lidded eyes, she undulated beneath him, her soft, panting breaths matching his. He could still taste her on his tongue, could feel her hot core clenching around him, and he let himself drown in the moment he'd begun to doubt would ever happen.

It had been *so* worth the wait.

He had no experience at this, but his body knew what to do even if his mind didn't. Very slowly, he pumped his hips, hissing as her silken sheath rippled and contracted, squeezing his length with every leisurely thrust.

"You feel...incredible." Dropping to his elbows, he took her nipple between his lips and teased it with his tongue. She made the sexiest sounds when he did that, and she made an even sexier one, a breathy groan, when he scraped a fang over the plump swell of her breast.

Arching, she took him deep and clawed his back with her nails. Ah...damn, that was good. The pain and pleasure combined to make everything more intense as he moved against her, savoring every sensation. He wanted to spend forever like this, but after a hundred and forty years of celibacy, this felt too good. He knew he wouldn't last long.

He dropped his mouth to hers and kissed her with renewed

urgency. A sound broke from her, needy and passionate, as she wedged one hand between their writhing bodies and cupped his sac. Her fingers were magic, rolling his balls between them, pinching the taut skin.

Perspiration bloomed on his forehead and his blood pounded through his veins as he picked up the pace, his body taking over as his thoughts scattered.

"You're mine," he rasped. "Finally, you're mine."

"Zhubaal...Z...yes, oh, yes..." She arched, pressing her breasts against him and crushing his hips between her powerful thighs. "Now," she gasped. "I want to see you come."

Her words, her use of his casual nickname, all of it triggered a primal response, obliterating his ability to think. All he could do was feel as he lunged into her, pumping and churning, powerless to control his body as the orgasm crashed over him in a violent, euphoric tidal wave. His body bucked, reaching for another peak. It struck him before the first one died down, and when the third hit him, he was sure they'd been transported to Heaven again.

Oh, yeah, this was way better than the sad, single orgasms he had by himself.

Beneath him, Vex went full noodle, her legs falling to the sides, her arms splayed out on the mattress. "I don't think I can move," she breathed.

He collapsed beside her, his chest heaving, his skin damp with sweat. Damn, that had been beyond his expectations, which was saying something, since he'd been fantasizing about his first time since the day he'd popped his first erection.

"Well." Shifting so she was facing him, Vex twined their fingers together, and for some reason, that struck him as more intimate than anything they'd just done. Maybe because sex, even if considered an expression of love, still became about strict biology at some point in the act. Holding hands was about affection. Had she finally accepted the inevitability of their relationship? "Was it all you imagined?"

Closing his eyes, he brought her hand up to his mouth and pressed his lips to her knuckles. "It was more. Way more."

"So, what now? In your losing your virginity scenario, what happened next?"

Next? He'd never gotten past this part. Before Laura lost her wings, they'd been wed in his fantasies, but after that...

"Marry me," he blurted.

"What?" Vex blinked. "Whoa." She sat up, releasing him. "Slow down there, Slick."

Frowning, he propped himself on one elbow. "What's the matter? It's what we always wanted—" He cut himself off, realizing his mistake even as frost formed in her eyes.

"We?"

He winced. "I know, you don't remember." It was probably a good thing since Laura had wanted a big, frilly celebration, the thought of which had given him hives. Still did. "We have time to figure it out." He reached out and trailed his fingers along the seam of her legs where they were pressed together, remembering how they'd gripped him as he'd thrust inside her. Her inner thigh was wet with the evidence of their lovemaking, and his cock stirred again, eager to make another mess. No wonder people were so obsessed with sex.

It was awesome.

"You could move in with me," he said, because hey, he hadn't just humiliated himself enough by proposing before they'd even caught their breath.

"I might have to," she muttered, shifting so he had access to anything he wanted. He loved that about her, how freely she gave him her body and how unself-conscious she was. "Everything I have in the human world is being repossessed thanks to the soul market crash."

"Well, it's good that you won't be doing that kind of work anymore." He leaned over and kissed her thigh, tasting them both on her skin. "It's dangerous."

"It is," she hedged, nudging his head toward her core. Oh, yeah. "But that was my choice, and I don't regret it. I had to make a living, and it was either that or porn." He jerked his head up to stare at her. She grinned, but he wasn't amused. "What? Why are you making that judgey face again?"

He sat up, his desire dulled by the topic of Vex with other males. "There are things that are hard for me to accept," he said roughly. "I'm used to the Laura who wouldn't pull petals off a flower because it would damage them. To hear you talk about capturing souls and selling them, or starring in skin flicks...it's...hard to grasp."

She ran her hand through her sex-mussed hair, leaving even more spikes and grooves. "You said you didn't care about the porn. Was it okay because you didn't know my soul was also Laura's? But now that you know we're the same..."

"You didn't do any porn. I know you were teasing. My point is that Laura wouldn't have even teased. The subject would have been...unseemly...to her."

Vex barked out a laugh. "Oh, my God, Laura was a freaking prude. How could you stand her?"

Abruptly, anger replaced the last echoes of arousal, and he swung out of bed. "You don't know her. And you aren't even trying."

She sighed. "That's because you want me to be her, and as much as you wish I was, I'm not."

That wasn't true. Not really. But it would be nice if she would at least make an attempt to recall some of their life together. Or not make fun of it. "Don't you remember any of it?"

"Nothing." She hurled the word at him like a rock, and sure enough, it struck its mark and left a bruise.

"There are people we can see." His voice was clipped, his frustration evident as he yanked open his armoire and tossed a robe to the bed for her. "Demon psychics who could help you remember—"

"No." She swung her legs over the side of the bed and shoved to her feet. "Don't you get it? How many times do I have to say it? I'm not Laura. And I don't want to be Laura. I only know this life, the one given to me by parents who weren't perfect, but who I loved. Denying my life would be denying them. I like my life, Zhubaal."

"You like it?" Was she serious? She used to be an angel. An elite angel. Even if she wasn't very good at it. "You like being the generic offspring of two fallen angels? You like having so few abilities and little power?"

"You're one to talk." She snatched up the robe with an angry sweep of her hand. "Do you like being a fallen angel? Are you proud of the things you've done in the name of evil?"

He swiped a pair of sweat shorts from his drawer. "I did it for you."

"Oh, fuck off," she snapped, clutching the robe to her chest.

"You do *not* get to lay the blame for all of this on me. You did it for yourself. Maybe you sucked at being an Ipsylum and were looking for an excuse to get out of it. Or maybe you weren't happy with yourself and used Laura's fall from grace to avoid facing that fact. I don't know. But what I do know is that you need to understand that my name is Vex, not Laura. And I've done a lot of things Laura would probably never have done, and I'm not sorry. I told you I like my life, but apparently Laura didn't like hers."

"She loved her life," he shot back, but even as he said it, the words rang hollow, and Vex called him on it.

"Really?" she taunted him. "Because if Saint Laura was so happy, why was she so eager to give up being an angel? If she was so content, why didn't she marry you when she had the chance?"

He ground his teeth, vexed—literally—by the argument and the fact that he felt like he was losing it. "Ipsylum can't marry until they pass their fiftieth birthday. We had ten years to go when she was kicked out of the Order."

Sighing, she shook her head. "Look, maybe we should just relax for a while. Feel like a dip in the hot tub?" She tossed the robe on the bed once more before walking across the room and dipping a toe into the steaming water. "We can play *Hot Tub Time Machine*."

"Is that a sex game?" The thought that she might have played it with another male was enough to flip his jealousy switch again.

Laughing, she splashed at the water with her foot. "It's a movie. Something you might know if you had decent cable down here." She beckoned to him, making her breasts bounce hypnotically. "Come on. You can go first. If you could go back in time in your bubbling time machine, where would you go?"

"That's easy," he said with a shrug. "I'd go back a hundred years and stop you from losing your wings."

She'd started to get into the pool, but froze with one foot on the top step. "Excuse me?"

Her tone, so shocked and defiant, pissed him off. He'd understood why she'd resisted her past, but damn it, why was she so determined to completely deny who she used to be and who they were to each other?

"If I could go back in time, we wouldn't be in the situation we're in," he pointed out. "We'd be who we're supposed to be."

"You bastard," she whispered. "You *bastard!*" She wheeled around, her face mottled with fury. "You still don't get it, do you? You still think your precious Laura is perfect. But I have news for you, asshole. You might have made love to Laura, but it wasn't Laura who made love—no, I take that back. It wasn't Laura who *fucked* you. It was me. It wasn't Laura who has been living in the human and demon realms for the last thirty years, who grew up with parents she loved in a life that was happy. You want to erase all that? You want to erase *me?*"

"I don't want to erase you," he shouted. "I want you to...fuck, I don't know. I just can't understand how you didn't know about me. On some level, you should have felt that there was something missing in your life. That all those guys trying to get in your pants weren't the right ones." Bottled up anger rose like steam from the hot tub as he clenched his fists at his sides to keep himself from shaking sense into her. "I waited all this time for you. I *sacrificed my wings* for you. And what did you do? You bopped around your happy little life, fucking God only knows how many males, while I spent every waking moment of every day searching for you like a damned idiot!"

Tears shimmered in her eyes as she looked around, presumably for her clothes, but they'd been left in a ball on Rowan's floor. "So that's who you want me to be? The innocent, sweet, shy girl you say I was?" She stormed over to the bed and snatched up the robe again. "Because I can't be her. I can't be anything but me. I love you, but I won't change who I am for anyone." She tied the robe around her waist and spread her arms wide. "This is me. You either love me for who I am, or you find someone else to love. But either way, Laura is gone. And right now, so am I."

She slammed out of the room, leaving him alone with nothing but his memories and his misery.

Chapter Fourteen

Vex had been gone from Sheoul-gra for two days, and in that time, Zhubaal had done nothing but sit in his quarters and get drunk. Razr had come by twice, only to get empty alcohol bottles lobbed at his head. Lilliana had come by as well, but Z didn't let her in. Even Cat had tried to talk to him, but seeing how she was the only other female besides Laura/Vex he'd kissed...ever...he shut her down. He didn't need to be reminded of yet another romantic failure.

It wasn't until Azagoth sent word that Revenant was finally on his way that Zhubaal emerged from his quarters. On the bright side, his hangover was pretty mild.

Zhubaal approached the landing pad, surprised to find Lilliana already there. She didn't usually meet visitors, but hey, apparently he was clueless about females.

Light blasted the pad, and Revenant appeared, his massive wings extended as if he'd flown in. As the most powerful being in Sheoul, he could have flashed into Sheoul-gra, but he and Azagoth had worked out a deal of mutual respect, and as long as Azagoth toed the line, Revenant was willing to follow the rules and not squash them all like bugs.

Zhubaal liked that in a demigod.

Azagoth appeared next to Lilliana and greeted Revenant with a handshake. The King of Hell had changed his look since Z had seen him last. Sometimes he was bald, sometimes blond, but today his hair, waist-length and so black it hurt to look at, wasn't the change. Neither was the full suit of wicked-looking matte charcoal armor, the shoulders and elbows adorned with sharp spikes, all of which Z had seen before. But the black cape was new. It hung heavy, as if it were made of rubber, but only when he got closer did he realize that it definitely was not made of any common material.

Azagoth shook his head as he eyed the new addition to Revenant's wardrobe. "Capes are stupid. They're nothing but liabilities during a fight."

"Oh, hey," Lilliana said, elbowing her mate lightly in the ribs. "Don't say exactly what you're thinking or anything."

Revenant laughed. "He's an asshole, but he's right. Which is why this is no ordinary cape." He nodded at Z. "Grab it. I dare you."

Curious, but hoping he didn't get vaporized, Z reached for it, only to have it slip through his fingers as if it were nothing but air. But a moment later, his hand stung like he'd been bitten by a venomous fire imp.

"Damn," he breathed as he shook his hand out. "What the fuck is that?"

"It's made from the hide of a Darquethoth."

Lilliana winced. "Ew."

"Ah, don't shed a tear for him," Revenant said as he admired the cape. "He was a douchemonkey. He should have thought a little harder about betraying me." He turned around, and for a moment, he seemed to disappear from the neck to his boots. "Cool, huh? It repels magic and it's impenetrable by sharp objects and bullets. Everyone should have one."

"Aren't you immune to that stuff anyway?" Zhubaal asked.

He wagged his finger. "*Nearly* immune. A spear or bullet can impale me, but they won't kill me. It'll hurt like hell and piss me off, though." He glanced between the three of them. "So what am I here for? Azagoth said it was urgent. It better be, because I have a birthday party to go to."

"A birthday party?" Zhubaal wasn't quite sure he'd heard that right. The guy didn't seem like the cake and balloons type. "You go to birthday parties?"

"When it's for my niece and nephews, fuck yeah. There's always at least one brawl at Horsemen parties." He waggled his brows. "Good times."

"You'll have to tell me what they thought of my gift," Azagoth said, and his smirk was about as evil as it got.

"I'm afraid to ask." Lilliana sighed.

Zhubaal wasn't. "What did you send?"

Azagoth's green eyes sparkled with mischief. "I hired a clown. One of those summoned ones that wreaks havoc until you kill it." He shrugged. "I figured the least I could do would be to provide some entertainment."

"That's terrifying," Lilliana said, shooting her mate a glare.

Revenant laughed. "It's hilarious." He clapped Azagoth on the back. "Let's get this over with so I can get to the party and watch the show."

As Azagoth and Revenant flashed to what Z assumed would be Azagoth's office, he wondered why the hell he'd been required to greet Revenant. But when Lilliana gently laid her hand on his arm, he realized he'd been duped, and she was probably the architect of the dupery.

"Is everything okay?" she asked. "You've been locked away in your room, and Vex hasn't been back. We're all worried."

Worried? They were worried about him? No one but Laura had ever worried about him. Not even his parents. As pitiless and efficient warriors, Ipsylum took a survival-of-the-fittest approach to life, something he'd rejected as Laura fell further and further behind in their studies and training. Gradually, their brethren began to shun her. Z had stood by her side, helping where he could, cheating if he had to, all to keep her from being banished from their Order.

But when her own family cast her aside like an injured hell mare that couldn't keep up with the herd, he hadn't been able to protect her anymore. He'd fought like hell, fought until his bones were broken and his skin was blackened by holy fire, but Laura had been ripped away from him by the people they'd both trusted most.

"I'm fine," he lied. He wasn't even close to being fine. Every beat of his heart hurt, as if it didn't know why it was bothering to pump lifeblood through his dead body. He hadn't felt this way since Laura died, and in a way, this was even worse, because the female he loved was still alive. She just wasn't his.

"Zhubaal," Lilliana began as she steered him toward the courtyard fountain, "what happened between you and Vex?"

He'd just spent the last two days angry and drunk, convinced that their falling out was her fault, but right now, with a little clarity and more blood than alcohol in his veins, he'd freely admit that everything could be laid at his feet. Everything.

Humiliation made his skin shrink. "I screwed up," he said, despising himself more with each word. "I expected her to be something—some*one*—she's not. Then I rejected the person she is."

Lilliana reached out to run her fingers through the water as they walked past the fountain. "When I first came here, I did the same thing to Azagoth. I expected him to be a monster."

"I remember." He gave her the side-eye. "But he *was* a monster."

"He was," she agreed. "And in a lot of ways, he still is. But my point is that I knew what I was getting into, and I rejected him anyway because I didn't give him a chance." She stopped and turned to face him. "Did you give Vex any chance at all?"

He felt sick to his stomach, because no, he hadn't. He'd judged her based on memories colored by blind love and guilt. A lot of guilt. He'd always blamed himself for not being able to protect her from being banished, losing her wings, or getting slaughtered.

And then, once he found her again, he'd insisted that Vex wasn't the real her. That somehow, if he could just break through the outer Vex he'd find the inner Laura. He'd wanted her to be that sweet angel he'd loved, because if he could get her back, he could make amends and banish the guilt he'd been harboring for nearly a century. So in a way, he'd wanted to erase Vex, just like she'd said.

He'd been a selfish piece of shit.

How could he not have thought about how crappy her existence had been as Laura? He'd been the one good thing in her life. Now there were a lot of good things in her life, and he wasn't one of them.

Son of a bitch.

Now he got it. Now he knew why Azagoth hadn't told him that Vex was Laura. Vex was *not* Laura. She was Vex, just as he'd said. But at the time Zhubaal wouldn't have accepted it. He'd had to learn that on his own, and he had, but not before royally fucking it up immediately after making love to her for the first time.

"Zhubaal?" Lilliana prompted. "Did you give her a chance?"

"No," he croaked. "You know I didn't."

She reached into her jeans' pocket and pulled out a scrap of paper. "Before she left, we got her personal information. For employment purposes, of course." She winked. "She's even got a Facebook profile. Says she's single. You should probably go beg her forgiveness and then get her to change her status to *in a relationship*."

Z's heart gave a great, happy thump. "Thank you, Lilliana," he said. "I'm glad Azagoth found you."

Now he had to go find *his* mate. He just hoped he wasn't too late.

* * * *

The moment after Azagoth closed his office door, he poured Rev and himself a stiff whiskey, an expensive label given to him by Revenant's Horseman niece, Limos, and got down to business.

"The barriers that keep demon souls inside Sheoul-gra are failing," he said, handing a highball glass to the Shadow Angel, "and it's your fault."

"My fault?" He put the glass to his lips and watched Azagoth from over the rim. "Have I been killing so many of my enemies that you don't have room for them?" Revenant asked that question with a straight face and a deadpan voice, but Azagoth knew him well enough to know he was being sarcastic.

"No," Azagoth said, just as reasonably. "But nice job with that. You've sent me some real bastards to deal with."

"Thank you."

Ignoring Revenant's insincerity that only echoed Azagoth's own, he explained. "The problem," he began, "is that your policy of reincarnating only souls of lesser evil means that the Inner Sanctum is filling with highly malevolent demons, more than we've ever had to house at once. It's causing an instability in the containment system itself, and it's creating weak spots in the barriers. Demons who are in the right place at the right time, or who are evil and powerful enough to exploit the structural failures, are escaping." He was also taking a huge hit in business. Before Revenant's mandate, Azagoth had taken bribes of money, gifts, or favors in order to reincarnate high-level evil demons.

Even Heaven had taken notice of the instability in the Inner Sanctum, hence the visit from Jim Bob and Ricky Bobby. Oh, his Heavenly spies had come on other business as well, but Jim Bob had made it abundantly clear that the Archangels were starting to get their halos in a twist.

Revenant gazed into the fire, the flickering light casting shadows on his stern face. "You're going to have to find a way to shore up the barriers."

"Why? Why the fuck are you doing this?" Azagoth slammed his glass down on his desk and strode over to him. "Look, buddy, you're new to this, but I've been handling souls for thousands of years. I keep the Inner Sanctum and Sheoul balanced. That's always been the cornerstone of our Creator's vision. Balance. The human realm is a balance of good and evil, but it's weighted toward good. Sheoul is the exact opposite, weighted more heavily toward evil. If you mess with that, the results could be disastrous."

"Thank you for the lecture about the fine balance between good and evil," Revenant drawled. "It's not as if I run Hell or anything." He knocked back the rest of his drink, never taking his gaze off Azagoth. "You understand why I want only the lesser evil souls reincarnated and the more malevolent ones kept imprisoned, yes?"

"Actually, I'm not clear on that," Azagoth said bitterly. This was his turf, and he didn't appreciate being left out of the loop. "I've assumed it's because you're an angel, not a fallen angel, and you still have connections to Heaven. Or, you know, decency."

"Decency?" Revenant snorted. "Those Heavenly bastards can suck my dick. I don't care about them. What I care about is the fact that Satan's prison will only hold for a thousand years." He appeared to consider that. "Well, nine-hundred and ninety-nine now. It's a prophecy that can't be averted. When that evil hellratfuck bastard finally breaks free, it's foretold that Armageddon will begin."

"And you don't want him to have an army of evil at his fingertips." Revenant was smarter than Azagoth had given him credit for.

"Exactly. I might be the Grand Poobah of Hell, but that doesn't mean I want evil to win the ultimate battle of all battles."

It was sound thinking, but there was going to be a different kind of Armageddon happening if the Inner Sanctum's walls fell and billions of demon souls spilled out into Sheoul and the human realm.

"Bottom line," Azagoth said. "I can get mages and builders to reinforce the barriers, but there's only so much they can do. We need a release valve."

"Fine." Revenant waved his hand dismissively. "Reincarnate more Tier three, four, and five demons, but not in the same numbers Satan allowed. Cut by two-thirds."

Azagoth winced. He'd have preferred to cut only by a third, a half at the most, but he wasn't going to complain. This would go a long way toward easing the explosive pressure of evil in the Inner Sanctum, for a little while, at least.

"I have another matter." Azagoth spoke over the sound of a shriek coming from inside the closed soul tunnel. He hadn't opened it yet this morning, and the *griminions* and their wards were getting restless. Idiots. Where most of them were going was far, far worse than where they were now. "I need your goons to lay off one of my employees. She's a *daemani*, and she's collecting souls who escape through the rifts in the barrier." He glanced expectantly at Rev. "I assume you're behind the collapse of the soul market."

"Of course."

Figured. And it made sense. High-ranking Orphmages and Charnel Apostles had formed a coalition against Revenant, and their prime source of spell power was the life energy from souls. Rumor had it that they were devising a demon version of a nuclear weapon to use against Revenant, and the moment Revenant heard that, he'd crushed the infant insurgency in its cradle.

"So you'll make sure Vex is safe?"

Revenant inclined his head. "I'll get the word out."

Excellent. Now he just had to get Vex and Zhubaal back together. He hoped Lilliana made some headway already. He'd been rooting for the guy, had even done a little of his own investigating in an attempt to find Laura. But he believed in fate, and he didn't doubt that two souls who were meant for each other would always find their way back no matter how many lives it took to do it.

And speaking of souls, Azagoth launched into the final piece of business he wanted to discuss with Revenant. "Before you go, I do have one more little thing. A gift." Not out of the goodness of his heart, of course. Strings were definitely attached, and when the time came that he needed a favor, he'd yank those strings like a damned puppet master.

Revenant rubbed his hands together in glee. "I love presents. What is it?"

"The most recent escapee from the Inner Sanctum. I was going to punish her, but I thought she might be of some use to you. And if not, I'm sure you know someone who would salivate at the chance to make her existence hellish. A certain Horseman, maybe? All of them, since it's their birthdays? Or Harvester, perhaps?"

"I'm intrigued." Revenant's voice went low, dark, and pure predator.

Azagoth willed a section of his stone wall to slide open, revealing a female standing in a cage, her gaze defiant. Bold. Until she saw Revenant.

"Revenant," Azagoth said, "you might have already met my guest."

Revenant laughed, a deep, dark sound that made the female cower at the back of the cage. "This couldn't have happened on a more appropriate day." He moved toward her, slowly, a panther stalking a rabbit. "It's good to see you again, especially since your son killed you before I could do it. And he did it far quicker than I would have." With every step, she shook harder, until the cage's metal joints began to rattle. "But life and death is all about second chances, isn't it, Lilith?" His wings snapped up with a crack that shattered Azagoth's highball glass. "And don't worry. I'll be sure to tell the Horsemen their mother said happy birthday."

Chapter Fifteen

Vex was never getting on Facebook again. Happy people and their grammatically challenged memes annoyed the shit out of her.

She slammed her laptop shut and tucked it into her bag. Today was moving day. Azagoth had offered to send Memitim to help her move some of her belongings into her assigned quarters in Sheoul-gra, and they'd have an easy time of it because she really didn't have much she wanted to take. As long as her apartment was far away from Zhubaal's quarters, she'd be happy.

Hades's mate, a chick named Cat, had come by yesterday with paperwork for her new apartment, which shocked the hell out of Vex. Azagoth really did run his realm like a mayor, and apparently, Cat helped keep track of who lived where.

Memitim and Unfallen stayed in the dorms, Azagoth, Zhubaal, Razr, and a handful of Azagoth's most trusted staff lived in his palace, and all other servants lived in apartments in other buildings. And now, thanks to Zhubaal, everyone got basic cable and two movie channels. Which was awesome, because she'd die if she couldn't watch *Game of Thrones*. Now if she could just get *The Walking Dead*, leaving the human realm might not be so bad.

But there was no way she was going to deal with Zhubaal to get it.

Her heart clenched. How could she miss him so much when she'd only known him for a few days? Yeah, yeah, there was the whole bitchface Laura thing and their eternal, fated soul-mate bullshit, but she wasn't buying it.

Oh, the fact that her soul knew his had no doubt hasted her feelings along, but when she saw him in her mind, she wasn't seeing old memories. She was seeing him skipping a rock across a pond. She was seeing him laugh, the way his eyes sparkled and the muscles in his cheeks twitched as he smiled. She was seeing him kissing his way up her body and sheathing himself inside her for the first time, his expression filled with wonder at the tender intimacy they shared.

That was who she missed. Not the Zhubaal from some winged fairy tale life he'd said they'd had in Heaven.

A knock at the door startled her. The Memitim were here already? But no, when she opened the door, there were no earthbound angels standing on her porch. There was, however, a fallen angel she didn't feel like talking to on her porch.

"Go away." She slammed the door in his jerk face and turned, only to smack into his broad chest. Yelping in surprise, she leaped back. "Zhubaal! What the hell?"

Damn it, she knew she should have warded the house. Then she wouldn't have to look at his handsome face as he stood there in well-worn jeans, a T-shirt that did nothing to hide hard-cut abs, and a black leather jacket that probably concealed an arsenal of weapons.

"Vex, we need to talk."

"Oh, it's Vex now? Not Laura?" She brushed past him to grab her bag. If he wasn't leaving, she would.

"Please, Vex." He caught her by the arm and pulled her around. "Listen to me. I love you—"

She yanked out of his grip. "You love *Laura*."

"I *did* love Laura." He jammed his hands into his jeans' pockets and fixed his gaze somewhere behind her. "I loved her more than my own life. She was my world and my reason to live." His gaze focused and shifted, catching hers. "But she's gone. I understand that. And it's okay because I have you."

She gaped. It had all sounded great until that last bit. "So I'm a consolation prize? You can't have Laura so you'll settle for me?"

"What? No! Never." He gripped her shoulders and bent so they were eye to eye. "I've fallen in love with you *because* you're Vex. Not because I thought you were Laura. She's in the past now. I don't want what she and I had. I want what you and I *can* have. We just need time and to get to know each other."

Vex couldn't believe what she was hearing. Or maybe she was afraid to believe what she was hearing. "You mean, if Laura was standing right beside me, and you had to choose—"

"I'd choose you." He released her to pace around, jamming his fingers through his hair over and over. "God, Vex, I think I was so desperate to find Laura because I felt guilty about everything that had happened to her. And when I found you, I thought that if I could just get you to remember, I could somehow fix the past. But I was an idiot. We were so young when we made those promises to each other, but we've both grown into the people we should be. I'm not the person I was back then, either. You're not Laura, and I'm glad."

Tears spilled from her eyes, running down her cheeks in a stream. "Really?"

"Touch my soul, Vex." Stopping in front of her, he took one of her hands and pressed it over his heart. "On my honor, it's you I want. Only you. I would *never* erase you." His heartbeat pounded into her palm as if it agreed.

On the verge of sobbing, she tried to lighten the mood. She'd never been good at the mushy stuff, anyway. "We have to have sex for me to touch your soul, you know."

"I know." His smile was pure, masculine hunger, and she was just as starved.

"Take us to your place," she purred. "We're going to play Hot Tub Sex Machine."

"I thought it was *Hot Tub Time Machine*," he said, adding a wry, "I have a better answer this time."

Laughing, because he couldn't possibly have a *worse* answer than last time, she dragged her finger down his abs to the fly of his jeans. "This is the porn version. If you're okay with that, of course."

Sure as shit, he was.

* * * *

Zhubaal couldn't believe his good fortune.

An hour ago, he'd been at rock bottom, lost, angry, and a little hungover. Now he was sprawled on a bench in his hot tub, watching with admiration as Vex stepped into the water, her curvy body naked and waiting for him to do naughty things to it.

He might not have a lot of experience, but he'd had a long fucking time to fantasize, so he figured there wouldn't be much of a learning curve. And even if there was, well, his Ipsylum instructors said he'd always been an enthusiastic student and a quick study.

He'd kissed her senseless and teased her before they'd stripped, and even now, as she moved toward him, her eyes were glazed with passion. Passion he'd put there. And now he understood that no matter how many lovers she'd bedded in the past, *he* was the one who had ripped off her panties with his teeth and whispered erotic things against the glistening flesh between her thighs. *He* was the one who had put her at the brink of orgasm when he tasted her breast with his fangs, drawing tiny twin droplets of blood that didn't come close to sating his hunger. And *he* would be the only one to do any of that ever again.

He took his straining erection in his fist and stroked, getting a kick out of that little catch in her breath as she watched him under the water. He pumped faster, adding a twist at the head, and she licked her lips. Oh, yeah, he could get used to having control over her like this, to rendering her speechless—

"I'm so going to suck on that."

He nearly choked on his own tongue. Damn, he loved how audacious, uninhibited, and unpredictable she was. It caught him off guard...and kept him from getting too cocky.

Planting one knee on either side of his hips, she wrapped her arms around his shoulders and sank down on his lap. Her folds cradled his shaft as she settled in and captured his mouth with hers.

There was nothing sweet and lingering about this kiss. No, this was raw and hot, punishing him for being a total ass while stoking the fire between them. She battled him with her tongue, nipped his lip and drew blood, rocked on his lap so his cock ground against her sex in the slippery water. He moaned as she raked his shoulders and neck with her nails and rubbed her breasts against his chest.

She was a master at balancing pain with pleasure, but he had a feeling she was letting the balance tip slightly in favor of pain this time.

Not that he was going to complain—hell, he was going to beg her to do it harder.

Abruptly, she pulled back. "Wanna see how long I can hold my breath? Because I'm a champ." Grinning, she slid off his lap like a wet seal and spread his legs, going to her knees between them at the bottom of the tub, so deep that the water came up to her chin.

"Vex—"

She ducked her head under water and swallowed his cock in one glorious motion. Holy...*fuck, yeah.* He hissed in surprise and pleasure as she sucked him deep and lashed him with her tongue. This was the first time a female had put her mouth on him like that. The sensations were unbelievable, beyond anything he could possibly have imagined. Vex's lips and teeth were magic, working together to deliver more of her pleasure/pain punishment.

Harder.

As if she'd heard his mental plea, she nipped his crown and pinched his balls, and he shouted in ecstasy.

She soothed him with a pump of her fist and gentle suck before taking him deep again. Hot water swirled around him as her tongue swirled around the head of his cock, and okay, she'd been right about sex in a hot tub.

These things were made for it.

With a final lick across the tip of his dick, she popped her head out of the water, her grin as impish as when she'd went under. "If you liked that, move over to the top step."

He narrowed his eyes at her. "What are you doing?"

She pushed the button on the side of the tub and the jets roared to life as she nudged him with her foot. "Hot Tub Sex Machine, remember?"

Best. Answer. Ever.

He did as he was told, moving to the other side of the tub. Sitting on the top step, the hot water just covered his thighs and the foamy bubbles lapped at the sensitive spot at the base of his shaft. His cock jutted out of the water, and knowing Vex liked to watch, he took it in his hand while she positioned herself in front of him, bent over, hands braced on his spread thighs. His erection gave an excited jerk. What was she doing?

A teasing smile tipped up her mouth as she dropped her head and lifted her ass so one of the jets struck her between her legs. Closing her eyes, she moaned, and he damned near came before her lips even touched his throbbing erection.

Holy shit. Zhubaal had never seen anything so erotic in his life as Vex as she tongued the slit at the tip of his cock and pumped her hips, fucking the hot jet. Opening her mouth over his crown, she took him deep and sucked upward so hard his hips came out of the water. As he sank back down, she slid her hand under him so her palm cradled his balls and her fingers tickled the seam of his ass.

Second only to finding Vex, this was the greatest moment of his life. He drowned in bliss, captivated by the motion of her head in his lap and how every once in a while, she'd look up at him with the fucking sexiest expression on her face. She was loving this as much as he was, and the sounds she made...sweet hell.

Her mouth worked harder and her hips pumped faster as she rode the jet. He threaded his fingers through her hair, the wet strands sticking up in wild spikes. The style suited her, sassy and colorful, short and sexy.

But nothing was as sexy as the way her skin flushed and her cries of passion went deeper as she neared climax. On the verge himself, he wanted to push her over the edge. Shifting, he angled himself so he had better reach and more range of movement. He slid his hands down her slippery body to her ass and lower, letting his fingers spread her wide and totally open to the powerful jet stream.

She cried out as she took the full force of the water. At the same time, ripples of pleasure cascaded through him, and he shouted as he came in a searing blast of heat. The sight of her swallowing his hot flow sent him into orbit again, but he wasn't done. Even as he came down from his second orgasm, he lifted her away from him, spun her around, and bent her over the side of the hot tub.

"Oh, my," she breathed as he shoved her forward and off her feet so she didn't have any purchase, leaving her vulnerable to whatever he wanted to do to her. They'd made love before, in bed, going slowly, but deep down he'd sensed that racier, frenetic sex was more her style, and frankly, he was pretty sure it was his, as well.

She gasped as he spread her wide with his thumbs and speared her with his tongue. He ate at her wet sex like he was starving, licking and sucking until she was whimpering with need. "Please...Z..."

Her moan was the most powerful aphrodisiac ever, and he gave her one more lingering thrust of his tongue deep inside her before replacing it with his cock in one powerful stroke.

She fit him like a glove, tight and warm, her satin walls contracting around him in waves from the base of his cock to the tip.

"Fuck," he breathed, holding himself rock-steady for a moment, afraid he'd blow if he moved.

He gripped her hips tight to keep her motionless, but it wasn't long before she started to squirm. Feeling a little sadistic, he waited a few more heartbeats, forcing her to wriggle more as her body sought what it needed.

When her needy curse echoed through the room, he couldn't take it anymore as his sexual instincts that demanded he satisfy his female screamed to the surface.

He pounded into her, the pace growing more frenzied with every passing second as she lay beneath him, utterly helpless against his every whim and every change in tempo. The sound of skin slapping skin joined the rhythmic splashing of the waves they were creating against the side of the pool. This was incredible...so fucking amazing...

Pressure built in his shaft, until it felt like his balls were boiling and his blood was steaming. His wings shot up and out as he threw back his head and roared as he came in a blinding blackout of ecstasy.

Vaguely, he felt her clench around him, milking him with her orgasm. The room spun as he bucked against her, riding the climax that seemed to go on forever. He filled her with his stream, his body jerking as his cock grew sensitive and his muscles turned to liquid.

Unable to support his own weight any longer, he collapsed on top of her, catching his upper body with his wings. Holy shit. He wasn't going to be able to walk for a week. Maybe they could just stay here and alternate between the bed and the hot tub. Maybe the shower, too. The things they could do with soap and the detachable shower head...

Vex stroked the long edge of one wing, and a freakishly potent sizzle of lust shot straight to his groin. "Are these sensitive?"

"They never were before," he mumbled against her slender shoulder. "I guess they get that way during sex."

She pressed her lips against the leathery skin, and he shivered with unexpected pleasure. "Well," she said between panting breaths, "if they are in any way sexual, we're gonna use 'em somehow."

It should have been impossible for him to get hard again, but...nope. Now his head was full of fantasies involving Vex and the tips and arches of his wings.

Gently, he lifted off her and drew her into his arms as he settled down in the hot tub with her seated next to him, her legs draped across his lap as she snuggled against his chest.

"Thank you." She pressed a lingering kiss to his neck.

Closing his eyes, he idly caressed her leg. "For what?"

"For accepting me for me."

He couldn't believe he almost hadn't. He'd been so damned stuck in a vow and the past that he couldn't see what was in front of him. Vex was magnificent, and he'd nearly thrown her away.

"The first time we made love," he rasped, "I was with Laura. This time, I was with you, Vex. I gave my virginity to Laura like I promised I would, but everything else, for the rest of eternity, belongs to you."

All this time, he'd been looking for an angel, but what he'd found was his soul.

And even better, he'd found its mate as well.

* * * *

Also from 1001 Dark Nights and Larissa Ione, discover Azagoth and Hades.

Sign up for the 1001 Dark Nights Newsletter
and be entered to win a Tiffany Key necklace.

There's a contest every month!

Go to www.1001DarkNights.com to subscribe!

As a bonus, all subscribers will receive a free
1001 Dark Nights story
The First Night
by Lexi Blake & M.J. Rose

Turn the page for a full list of the
1001 Dark Nights fabulous novellas...

Discover 1001 Dark Nights Collection Three

HIDDEN INK by Carrie Ann Ryan
A Montgomery Ink Novella

BLOOD ON THE BAYOU by Heather Graham
A Cafferty & Quinn Novella

SEARCHING FOR MINE by Jennifer Probst
A Searching For Novella

DANCE OF DESIRE by Christopher Rice

ROUGH RHYTHM by Tessa Bailey
A Made In Jersey Novella

DEVOTED by Lexi Blake
A Masters and Mercenaries Novella

Z by Larissa Ione
A Demonica Underworld Novella

FALLING UNDER YOU by Laurelin Paige
A Fixed Trilogy Novella

EASY FOR KEEPS by Kristen Proby
A Boudreaux Novella

UNCHAINED by Elisabeth Naughton
An Eternal Guardians Novella

HARD TO SERVE by Laura Kaye
A Hard Ink Novella

DRAGON FEVER by Donna Grant
A Dark Kings Novella

KAYDEN/SIMON by Alexandra Ivy/Laura Wright
A Bayou Heat Novella

STRUNG UP by Lorelei James
A Blacktop Cowboys® Novella

MIDNIGHT UNTAMED by Lara Adrian
A Midnight Breed Novella

TRICKED by Rebecca Zanetti
A Dark Protectors Novella

DIRTY WICKED by Shayla Black
A Wicked Lovers Novella

A SEDUCTIVE INVITATION by Lauren Blakely
A Seductive Nights New York Novella

SWEET SURRENDER by Liliana Hart
A MacKenzie Family Novella

For more information, go to www.1001DarkNights.com.

Discover 1001 Dark Nights Collection One

FOREVER WICKED by Shayla Black
CRIMSON TWILIGHT by Heather Graham
CAPTURED IN SURRENDER by Liliana Hart
SILENT BITE: A SCANGUARDS WEDDING by Tina Folsom
DUNGEON GAMES by Lexi Blake
AZAGOTH by Larissa Ione
NEED YOU NOW by Lisa Renee Jones
SHOW ME, BABY by Cherise Sinclair
ROPED IN by Lorelei James
TEMPTED BY MIDNIGHT by Lara Adrian
THE FLAME by Christopher Rice
CARESS OF DARKNESS by Julie Kenner

Also from 1001 Dark Nights

TAME ME by J. Kenner

For more information, go to www.1001DarkNights.com.

Discover 1001 Dark Nights Collection Two

WICKED WOLF by Carrie Ann Ryan
WHEN IRISH EYES ARE HAUNTING by Heather Graham
EASY WITH YOU by Kristen Proby
MASTER OF FREEDOM by Cherise Sinclair
CARESS OF PLEASURE by Julie Kenner
ADORED by Lexi Blake
HADES by Larissa Ione
RAVAGED by Elisabeth Naughton
DREAM OF YOU by Jennifer L. Armentrout
STRIPPED DOWN by Lorelei James
RAGE/KILLIAN by Alexandra Ivy/Laura Wright
DRAGON KING by Donna Grant
PURE WICKED by Shayla Black
HARD AS STEEL by Laura Kaye
STROKE OF MIDNIGHT by Lara Adrian
ALL HALLOWS EVE by Heather Graham
KISS THE FLAME by Christopher Rice
DARING HER LOVE by Melissa Foster
TEASED by Rebecca Zanetti
THE PROMISE OF SURRENDER by Liliana Hart

Also from 1001 Dark Nights

THE SURRENDER GATE By Christopher Rice
SERVICING THE TARGET By Cherise Sinclair

For more information, go to www.1001DarkNights.com.

About Larissa Ione

Air Force veteran Larissa Ione traded in a career as a meteorologist to pursue her passion of writing. She has since published dozens of books, hit several bestseller lists, including the New York Times and USA Today, and has been nominated for a RITA award. She now spends her days in pajamas with her computer, strong coffee, and fictional worlds. She believes in celebrating everything, and would never be caught without a bottle of Champagne chilling in the fridge…just in case. After a dozen moves all over the country with her now-retired U.S. Coast Guard spouse, she is now settled in Wisconsin with her husband, her teenage son, a rescue cat named Vegas, and her very own hellhound, a King Shepherd named Hexe.

For more information about Larissa, visit www.larissaione.com.

Discover Larissa Ione

Azagoth: A Demonica Underword Novella by Larissa Ione, Now Available

Even in the fathomless depths of the underworld and the bleak chambers of a damaged heart, the bonds of love can heal...or destroy.

He holds the ability to annihilate souls in the palm of his hand. He commands the respect of the most dangerous of demons and the most powerful of angels. He can seduce and dominate any female he wants with a mere look. But for all Azagoth's power, he's bound by shackles of his own making, and only an angel with a secret holds the key to his release.

She's an angel with the extraordinary ability to travel through time and space. An angel with a tormented past she can't escape. And when Lilliana is sent to Azagoth's underworld realm, she finds that her past isn't all she can't escape. For the irresistibly sexy fallen angel known as Azagoth is also known as the Grim Reaper, and when he claims a soul, it's forever...

* * * *

Hades: A Demonica Underworld Novella by Larissa Ione, Now Available

A fallen angel with a mean streak and a mohawk, Hades has spent thousands of years serving as Jailor of the Underworld. The souls he guards are as evil as they come, but few dare to cross him. All of that changes when a sexy fallen angel infiltrates his prison and unintentionally starts a riot. It's easy enough to quell an uprising, but for the first time, Hades is torn between delivering justice — or bestowing mercy — on the beautiful female who could be his salvation...or his undoing.

Thanks to her unwitting participation in another angel's plot to start Armageddon, Cataclysm was kicked out of Heaven and is now a fallen angel in service of Hades's boss, Azagoth. All she wants is to redeem herself and get back where she belongs. But when she gets trapped in Hades's prison domain with only the cocky but irresistible Hades to help her, Cat finds that where she belongs might be in the place she least expected...

Forsaken By Night

By Larissa Ione
Blood Red Kiss Anthology

Good things always come in threes—and this paranormal romance anthology featuring steamy stories from *New York Times* bestselling authors Kresley Cole, Larissa Ione, and Gena Showalter is no exception!

Get ready for a collection chock full of vamps, demons, aliens, and plenty of sizzle!

In Kresley Cole's celebrated story "The Warlord Wants Forever," the first in her scorching Immortals After Dark series, vampire warlord Nikolai Wroth will stop at nothing to claim his Bride, the one woman who can make his heart beat again. But can beautiful Myst the Coveted accept an enemy vampire as her own?

Tehya has spent the last twelve years as an accidental wolf, but is truly a vampire at heart. When she gets injured, Lobo sneaks her inside MoonBound's headquarters and nurses her back to health…with potentially deadly consequences. Desire collides with danger in "Forsaken by Night," a MoonBound Clan novella from Larissa Ione!

In Gena Showalter's Otherworld Assassins novella, Dark Swan, Lilica Swan isn't quite human or otherworlder; she is the best—and worst—of both. She is willing to do whatever proves necessary to save her sister from the seductive and deadly Alien Investigation and Removal agent, Dallas Gutierrez, even bond her life to his…effectively wedding him. But without consummation, the bond will fade. Can Dallas resist his insatiable desire for the powerful beauty? Or will she lead to his ultimate downfall?

* * * *

She was the woman he'd seen so many times in his mind.

Her slender shoulders rose and fell with each panting, exhausted breath, and she was shivering, but her amber eyes gleamed with recognition.

"You know me," Lobo said, his voice tight with astonishment and confusion. Who was she? Why was she here? It was all he could do to keep from blurting out every question at once.

She opened her mouth as if to speak, and he caught a glimpse of fangs. She was a vampire. A born vampire as well, or her eyes would be silver.

A blast of hunger hit him in a wave that was almost physical. Desperate need billowed from her, as if she was not only hungry, but chronically starved.

"Hey," he said gently. "I've got packets of human blood—"

She threw herself at him so suddenly he didn't have time to block her. In an instant, she was wrapped around him like a bear cub scaling a tree, and crazily enough, his first instinct wasn't to throw her off him.

His instinct was to hold her tighter and tilt his head to give her better access to his vein.

Lobo held the strange female against him, his body responding like a traitor as she sank her fangs into his throat. Pain and pleasure rippled through him, leaving him so unsteady that he had to brace himself against the wall. Ah, damn, this was good. Bizarre, but good.

He hadn't fed a female in long time, and he had definitely never fed a strange female who showed up at his door, naked and bloody.

But she wasn't a complete stranger, was she? He'd never met her, but he knew her. He'd seen her in his mind and in his dreams. Hell, she'd even made it into some of his fantasies, the ones that sometimes woke him in the middle of the night and left him drenched in sweat and painfully hard. And how many times had he summoned her image while he stroked himself in the shower?

As if she read his thoughts, she rocked against him, rubbing her bare chest against his, her pelvis against his rapidly hardening erection.

"Hey," he said roughly, as he tightened his hold in an attempt to calm her, but the only thing that did was bring her even more solidly against him. "It's okay. You can slow down."

If she heard him, she didn't respond. Keeping his grip on her, he sank onto the bed, knowing that at the rate she was feeding, it wouldn't be long before he got light-headed.

She took an extremely hard pull, and a burst of extreme pleasure-pain shot through him. "Jesus," he whispered. "How long has it been since you last fed?"

Her only response was a moan and a slow grind of her hips, which dredged up a moan of his own. This was like one of those erotic tales in a men's magazine, the insane ones that had to be fiction. Because seriously, who opens their door in the middle of nowhere to find a hot, naked, horny woman standing there?

Dear Hustler, have I got a story for you…

Her fingernails dug into his shoulders, creating sizzling pops of pain that heightened all his senses. He became aware of the way her breath tickled his skin. The way her hard nipples pressed into his chest. The way her sex rocked against the bulge beneath his fly. His hands shook as he gripped her waist, but what he really wanted was to slip his fingers between their bodies, release his cock, and drive into her the way he did it in his dreams.

But he couldn't do it. She was clearly suffering from feeding deprivation, leaving her vulnerable and too easily swayed. So he kept his hands safely where they were as she moved against him, feeding with increasing fervor. The scent of her arousal surrounded him, chipping away at his willpower.

Heat consumed him as she rode his erection, making little sounds of ecstasy with every back and forth sweep across his lap. He could feel her pleasure mounting, could practically taste in as an electric bite in the air.

She stiffened and clamped down on his throat hard with a throaty shout, and he damned near lost it in his pants.

As she disengaged her fangs and went limp, he eased them onto their sides, and for the first time since she'd burst into his cabin, he got a good look at her face. High cheekbones, flush with color, sloped gracefully to her hairline, and remarkably long lashes framed drowsy, sated yellow-amber eyes that drilled into him not with their intensity, but with their familiarity. He knew those eyes…but from more than just the visions. Why?

"I guess maybe I should get your name now…"

On behalf of 1001 Dark Nights,

Liz Berry and M.J. Rose would like to thank ~

Steve Berry
Doug Scofield
Kim Guidroz
Jillian Stein
InkSlinger PR
Dan Slater
Asha Hossain
Chris Graham
Pamela Jamison
Jessica Johns
Dylan Stockton
Richard Blake
BookTrib After Dark
The Dinner Party Show
and Simon Lipskar

53176709R00087

Made in the USA
Lexington, KY
26 June 2016